Blood of the Innocent

A Novel

I0548251

Saa Maurice Sindondoeh Jumu

Sierra Leonean Writers Series

Blood of the Innocent

ISBN: 978-9988-8743-7-7

Sierra Leonean Writers Series
Warima/Freetown/Accra
120 Kissy Road, Freetown, Sierra Leone
Kofi Annan Avenue, North Legon, Accra, Ghana
Publisher: Prof. Osman Sankoh (Mallam O.)
publisher@sl-writers-series.org
www.sl-writers-series.org

Dedication

This book is dedicated to the following:

My wife, Halima Sedia Jumu (Lecturer, Milton Margai College of Education and Technology),

My children; Betty, Kasay, Tambay and Hannah Holima
My grandchildren, Jamestina and Halima Sesay
The entire Jumu family

Acknowledgments

My sincere thanks go to the following people:

My late mother, Sia Hawa Jumu, popularly known as Koboeh, for her storytelling lessons that kept the fire burning in me to write my own stories.

The entire farming community in Kambaya, for the animated storytelling sessions which was organized for the neighborhood children, including me.

My late uncle, Komba Jumu, nicknamed Okonkwo, a retired Military Serviceman, who helped to lay my educational foundation.

Mr. Alan Davison, for making literature very interesting to me at Jaiama Secondary School.

Mr. D. H. Wilkes, for encouraging me to read many novels
Haja kadie Kamara and Bai Tejan Kargbo, for typing the Manuscripts.

Messers Komba David Sandi, Harry O. T. Lebbie and Emmanuel Senessie for editing the Manuscripts

My special thanks to my Publisher Prof Osman Sankoh (Mallam O of SLWS) and his staff.

Chapter One

The Intruder

The peace of Kambaya was disturbed. There was a rifle shot right in the center of the town, creating panic in the neighbourhood. The jubilant voices of children playing in the sand at the edge of the town ceased instantly. It was followed by a mad rush into the nearby houses as if another war had begun.

A group of men armed with rifles and sticks surrounded an old mango tree which stood tall and big in the center of the town. A sizeable crowd had gathered there, drawn by the shot.

The crowd surrounded the tree and stared curiously at its leafy branches in complete silence.

There was hardly any noise around except for the wind which blew across the town and shook the leaves violently, causing the extremely dry ones to drop to the ground.

Suddenly, a branch of the tree moved downwards, almost to breaking point as a big black object surged upwards in a flash. The movement was so fast that they could not see it but the movement of the leaves provided the direction of the action.

"Ay....Ay!" come this way, it is here" shouted an onlooker.

A man with a rifle rushed briskly to the point where he stood and looked up. He did not see anything and then looked at the man doubtfully to show his disappointment. But the man was convinced that he saw an object and so

1

he broke the silence again. "Yes, I saw an object, I am not lying," he said aloud trying to convince the rifle man, who waved his hand frantically in an effort to keep him quiet. He understood the sign and kept quiet but continued to stare at the leaves to prove that the object was there.

Walking round the tree in circles with a systematic and cautious movement of their feet, with their eyes fixed on the tree top, looked like some sort of a ceremony.

The search became tiresome but as the rays of the rising sun threw more light into the obscurity created by the leaves and the branches, the crowd was hopeful to find the intruder.

Kaimoto, looking rather impatient, folded his trousers up to his knees and passed over his neck the belt of the rifle which was attached to the nozzle and butt.

Then he hung unto a branch of the tree and pulled himself upwards. Within a few minutes he had gone halfway through the distance to the top and sat on a big branch. He removed the belt from his neck and hastily pointed the rifle at the tree top where the leaves were constantly shaking. He hurriedly took aim and within a split second there was an explosion that echoed throughout the town. The cartridges broke the branch on which the object sat and it lost its balance and fell on him. All three landed on the ground with a boom right in the center of the crowd. He crawled away quickly with his rifle fearful of the big black object which turned out to be a giant chimpanzee.

It lay flat on its back until an onlooker took a step closer. It rolled its bulky body over quickly and stood face to face with him. The crowd saw the confrontation and the imminent danger of a shootout.

It looked left, right and backwards trying to locate an

escape route but it realized it was in the middle of the crowd.

Then, a man with a long wooden pole, raised high above his head, came from behind it and struck with all his might. The primate skillfully avoided the blow and held unto the pole from the other end and pulled it harder. The man felt a great force exerted on the pole and let go of it quickly and ran for his life.

The crowd moved backwards when it took complete control of the pole. As the crowd moved further away it saw a safe passage which led to the main door of a house which it entered without any hesitation.

A woman and a teenager, horrified and speechless, ran out of the house on seeing the chimpanzee in one corner of the room. Then a young lady screamed when she realized that her baby was sleeping in the same house occupied by the chimpanzee. "Oh my child," she shouted repeatedly with her hands raised above her head, with tears in her eyes.

A rifle man came out of the crowd as a result of the appeal and went towards the house and cocked his rifle. He listened well and noticed that it was in another room different from where the child was. He went in quickly and brought the child out by his left hand whilst his right hand remained firmly on the trigger. The young woman breathed a sigh of relief and took the child away to the back of the crowd and forced the nipple of her breast into its mouth to keep it quiet.

Next, a hunting dog was brought and sent into the house while the riflemen took positions around it. The dog barked endlessly and entered the various rooms apparently chasing it.

The movement in the house became turbulent. There were tingling sounds of dishes and metal spoons as they fell to the ground. Then there was an encounter which lasted only a few minutes. The dog's barking turned into wailing. The dog came out limping with a broken tail and moved sluggishly across the road and licked its wounds, groaning. The crowd marveled at the dog's predicament.

Then, an elderly man came out of the crowd and ran quickly to his house and returned with hot burning coals in a coal pot. He went back there and came with a cup of dried pepper and turned its whole content into the burning coal. "Take this inside and it will come out," he said to the rifleman who stood close by him.

He cocked his rifle and took the pot of burning coal with his left hand and went to the door. He opened it slightly, placed the pot on the floor and closed it.

As the pepper burnt, the Chimpanzee could be heard moving from one room to another as the smoke of burning pepper filled the house.

The crowd looked on with anxiety, certain to hear the cracking sounds of the rifles and the sudden death of the chimpanzee. And in the twinkling of an eye its head appeared and disappeared again in the door way. The riflemen pulled their triggers halfway through and held their breath to ensure that the aim was on target but it disappeared quickly.

A few seconds later it came out because it could no longer put up with the smell of the burning pepper. All rifles pointed at it but suddenly a young lad appeared behind it, coughing and sneezing as he had been sleeping in the house. The crowd shouted in fear and the riflemen quickly withdrew their rifles. The chimpanzee moved swiftly into the nearby bush and disappeared.

Kaimoto followed the chimpanzee deep into the forest. The other riflemen stopped at the outskirts of the town and concluded that a chimpanzee in the forest was like a fish in the sea. Kaimoto moved quickly between the trees, across rivers and valleys ahead of it. The walk was tedious and long but he arrived at a point where there was a break in the forest chain. A big tree that provided the link was cut down and shredded into pieces of boards for commerce.

He selected a hideout and waited patiently. As he waited and sweated in the hideout, there was no sign of the chimpanzee anywhere. Could it have chosen another path? He asked himself over and again. As he raised his hand to wipe sweat from his face, he heard an unusual movement on his side. When he turned to see what was happening, he discovered a big black snake feeding on a decaying pineapple.

The snake cautiously dipped its head in and out of a hole on the side of the decaying pineapple. It stopped the process and scanned the environment with curiosity. He became stiff as he watched the head of the snake pointed at him and at a close range. He could feel sweat running down from his upper body to his limbs. A few things ran through his mind: to move out quickly or to use his machete. He could do neither of these things because the snake was gazing at him directly. The power in his hand and feet had all gone. What remained of him was his powerful gaze to ensure he saw every movement of that deadly snake.

Suddenly, a flower bird flew overhead and sat on a branch close to the decaying pineapple. It flew to a higher branch on seeing the snake and burst into a chat - chat-

chat sing song. It flew across on the other side shaking the leaves violently, and flew back to its original position.

Disturbed, the snake started to move its long body away, still gazing at the bird that kept coming closer.

At a point in time the bird came so close that the snake struck but missed as it flew quickly to a higher branch and avoided the blow.

The snake then continued its movement away from the pineapple and disappeared completely into the bush. And without wasting time, it flew and sat on the decaying pineapple and plunged its beak into the hole on the side and sucked the fluid.

With the snake no longer in view, he got up and walked quickly out of his hideout. The little bird heard the movement, drew its beak out of the pineapple and flew across the plains.

He gazed at it in flight. "Come back, come back, my little savior and have a field day to yourself", he said aloud in his mind.

The chimpanzee, after resting enough arrived at the point where it must come down from the trees and go through the shrubs before it could continue its journey up in the trees on the other edge. It peeped down on the ground, but could see nothing strange to prevent it coming down.

Kaimoto lay down close to the base of a big tree and heard quite clearly the noise it made.

His rifle was cocked and ready for action. His machete laid close by him in case its use became necessary. As a matter of fact, he was quite prepared for any confrontation as long as he was going to kill the primate at the end.

It hung on a branch which oscillated with it until it

jumped down on another tree.

He looked up and saw it from the side and he waited until he had a clear view of its head. And that moment came quickly. There was an explosion of rifle fire and a loud scream of pain from it.

It fell at the foot of the tree and struggled desperately breaking anything that came into its grips and tearing apart anything that it could bite. It struggled for a long time and laid flat on the ground at the foot of the tree.

He loaded his rifle again and cocked it. He moved cautiously towards the primate and touched it with the barrel. It jumped up and held unto it and tried to pull it away but he put up a fierce resistance as it was a matter of life and death. The struggle continued for some time until the barrel pointed at its chest. He released the trigger and there was another explosion of rifle fire that sent the chimpanzee backwards. It fell and struggled until it became motionless. He got up and loaded his rifle and repeated the process to prove whether it was dead or alive. This time around it did not respond to the touch of the barrel. It was dead and lay motionless at the foot of the tree.

He cleared the bush around it and prepared a carrier. He cut the hands, feet and the private parts for Sanugu who made a special request for them. He did not say why he needed the parts but his colleague hunter once told him in secret that he used chimpanzee or human parts or a combination of both in the concoctions which his clients use for fame, wealth or political power.

After resting twice along the thorny road, he finally came back home under the cover of night and under the heavy weight of the animal.

A hay of smoke hung over Madina town. Every

household was preparing some food in the kitchen for breakfast. A combination of different sweet smells of fried chicken, goat meat and fish made Madina quite a likeable place to live. The breakfast varied from day to day depending on the type of work at hand. For a ploughing day the breakfast would be heavy like for a brushing day. Typically, Madina was a farming village with very few traders. The traders too had backyard gardens that were big enough to make a significant contribution to their meals. Indeed Madina was fully engaged and its citizens enjoyed all the benefits of hard work. The children were joyful and healthy and peace reigned in the town.

Mattu prepared a heavy breakfast although there was hardly any hard work at hand. She explained to Brima her husband that lunch would he delayed because she and their daughter Panga would be going to Baudu to assist in harvesting her friend's rice farm. She explained further that Benakie the kola merchant, a friend to the family slept in Madina on his usual kola purchasing trips and she thought it necessary to offer him breakfast.

He paid attention to her but he was a man of very few words and sometimes instead of speaking he would nod his head to mean that it was OK. And that was exactly what he did to her after a lengthy explanation about the journey and the breakfast.

"Can't you say something please," she queried.

He smiled and touched her on the shoulder and said

"You are always right, go in peace and don't be late," he said. She felt good. His touch reminded her of the first time she met him. He was full of smiles and very much excited but of very few words. She could still remember the words. "Do you love me and are you prepared to stay with me for life?" He had asked. Apart from these words she could not remember anything more significant. But his touch was always meaningful and symbolic.

On their first face to face encounter, he held her right hand for long, squeezing it in a way that conveyed quite a lot of messages. She enjoyed that method of communication better than the words that came out of his mouth.

She went into the kitchen and prepared two dishes and took them to the table where he and Benakie were already seated and gave them some water and two spoons. And as the two friends ate their breakfast, she and Panga withdrew to the kitchen and ate their share out there.

Panga was half her mother's size and she was full of smiles. She was short and good looking from every angle. Her breast size forced an early maturity on her which she was not even aware of and did not choose special playmates.

At a particular instance she was found playing with boys of her age and Mattu rebuked her. But she replied saying, "I am just playing with them. Is anything wrong playing with them?" She asked her mother.

Panga and Mattu were more than daughter and mother; they were good friends.

Immediately after having their breakfast the two friends said goodbye to Brima and Benakie and set out for Baudu.

Kaimoto got up from bed earlier than the rest of the members of his house. He invited a handful of his friends within the neighborhood to help him butcher the chimpanzee which he had killed the previous day. The animal was rotated over the fire set up for that purpose until the hair on it was completely burnt.

It was removed from the fire, placed on banana leaves and cut into lumps. The names of members to benefit from the meat were announced by Kaimoto and the lumps were wrapped according to the names and distributed to the people. The gift brought joy to the recipients because meat was very scarce in Kambaya because hunting was very difficult during the dry season. The dried leaves and sticks broke under the feet of hunters and the noise scared away animals. Nevertheless, a dish without meat or fish for a household for a long time was considered a shameful for the head of that family. That was why Kaimoto was highly appreciated in the community, especially when he gave out meat freely to his neighbours.

River Katay also dried up in the dry season, forcing fishes to migrate downstream to enter river Sumunji, causing scarcity of fish in Kambaya. The fish that was usually available was from towns situated by big rivers which were far away to the extreme west of the region. But by the time they were brought by fish traders into small villages and towns, they were already over dried and tasteless, making life difficult for house wives and other women.

To address the twin problems of meat and fish scarcity, the youths transformed themselves into trap hunters and marksmen. Kaimoto was one such marksman. Whenever a rifle shot was heard from the direction of his hunting trip the people became joyful and looked forward to getting some meat at home. He would not make any promises when he went out hunting but he lived to the expectation of the members of his community.

That morning when he made sure the meat went according to the names, he took his hunting bag to the back of the house. He opened it and took out the hands, feet and private parts of the chimpanzee. He wrapped them in a piece of cloth which he kept in his traveling bag. He took his bath and dressed up hastily for a trip to Seneun. He was just about to close the door when his wife Tenja appeared in front of the house. She carried a bundle of husk rice and some dried meat. She was from a neighbor's farm.

He received her warmly and took the bundle inside the store, and then drew her attention to the fresh chimpanzee meat in the biggest of the pots.

She went to the pot and examined the meat and thanked him for being a dedicated and hardworking husband. She then went to the kitchen, lit the wood and brought out some meat which was to be preserved. Before she got fully involved in the processing of the meat, he announced his trip to Seneum in a manner which was not convincing at all.

Tenja turned round and faced him squarely, "May I know why you are going to Seneum? If you don't give me a convincing answer, I will go with you", she said in an excited manner. He came closer to her and held her firmly by the shoulders. "Tenja, try to understand me. I love you so much that I cannot do anything that would disturb your peace. You know very well that we need money for Christmas and that is exactly the reason why I am going to Seneun," he said

She looked at him sharply and realized he was serious about what he was saying and allowed him to go, on the condition that he returned the same day.

Seneun was a big town with shops, offices and a court

11

house. It was also a market centre which was only five kilometers away from Kambaya and a very busy route indeed. In the morning, midday, or evening people were either carrying goods or bringing them from there.

There was yet another aspect of Seneun. There was the famous court siren, the sound of which went far and wide as a reminder of the court's sittings. It helped many to be in the court room on time.

He bid his wife farewell and began the journey with zeal. He was prepared to return no matter what. He loved his wife and sympathized with her a lot. They had been married for three years without any children. That was the devil in the detail, but he was hopeful that time was on their side.

As he walked towards Seneun he reflected on the animal parts and what his colleague hunter once told him about Sanagu, that he used a combination of chimpanzee and human parts to make concoctions for his clients. He wondered where he got the human parts from. Was he killing people secretly or going to the grave yard at night? He could not find answers to these questions but they engaged his mind whenever the name Sanagu was mentioned.

Sanagu was neither a farmer nor a wine tapper. He was a fortune teller or diviner and a king maker. He lived on his profession and he never lacked anything. He had a large clientele of men and women from far and wide. His house always had clients who paid in kind or in cash.

Kaimoto walked through five kilometers as fast as he could and happened to be one of the clients waiting on a bench in the verandah, amidst several other people. He waited until his turn came and he went into the room where Sanagu was waiting.

Sanagu sat on a mat right in the centre of an incommodious room. There were bottles on one side and white plastic containers on the other side. The room had a single wooden bed covered with a multi-colored bed sheet, close to the wall on the right hand side of the room.

Sanagu got up from the mat and greeted him and realized he was not a normal client but was there at his own request.

Kaimoto sat on one of the two chairs by the door and opened his bag and brought out the parts.

"Good. You have done very well. Can you get me some more?" asked Sanagu.

"Chimpanzees are now very scarce. It is only by luck that one can come across them," he said calmly.

Sanagu raised his pillow and uncovered some money from which he gave him one hundred thousand Leones ($20).

"You have done very well and you need every encouragement", he said

He could not believe his eyes. He kept the money in his pockets and shook his hand firmly, bid him farewell and walked out of the house.

He went into the market and bought a few items before he finally left for Kambaya.

Chapter Two

The Sacrifice

Sanagu saw many clients throughout the evening until night fall. He was tired but happy that his income was on an increase and his fame was growing. He was rated the best diviner in the region.

He was rarely seen in public because he was always busy in his bedroom working on something for a client who may be either waiting outside or was inside the room with him. He was a king maker and a solution to many problems, both social and economic.

He came to Seneun a long time ago and began his work of fortune telling or divining in a house in one corner of the town. After many years of hard work he built himself a house which was one of the best in the town. He was married to two wives, Indy and Sattu.

Indy was tall and about forty. She had a fine set of white teeth and always carried a smile on her face. She occupied herself with the clients; arranging their seats and announcing them to Sanagu as and when they appear. Apart from these she was the first wife on whose shoulders the management of the kitchen rested. Every morning she listed the items to be bought and oversaw the commencement of the cooking. She also listened well for the rather frequent calls from him to which she responded quickly. She had two children, Mba and Kuti, seven and five years and both of them girls. Indy and the two girls occupied a room next to Sanagu's. It was only when Indy was busy or absent that he would allow Sattu to carry out some duties. But even there, she was allowed to carry out only selected pieces of work that had nothing to do with his bedroom. Any piece of work in his bedroom was carried out by Indy.

Sattu had very little to do in the house apart from cooking. She was about sixteen and enjoyed the company of her friends much to the annoyance of Indy. At various times she had to beg her visitors to leave the house so that Sanagu would not know that such things happened. With her cooperation she succeeded in getting rid of her visitors both boys and girls. She tried to let her understand that she was a married woman with definite restrictions on her behavior. Indy spent time teaching her about what was required of her as a wife. She was like a mother to her, and when Sattu clearly understood Indy's kindness and love towards her, she behaved herself.

She became fond of Mba and Kuti to the extent that she slept with them in her bedroom, washed their dirty dresses and looked after them.

The last client for that day came at night which was not unusual. He stood in the verandah and waited, after tapping on the door a few times.

The key turned in the lock and when the door opened, a man stood there. Indy then led him to Sanagu's bedroom. He entered into bedroom and sat on a chair close to the door.

"I am Senga, born in Malenka town but spent my childhood in Fitia. I returned to Malenka when it was time to go to school. After completing school, I have been in Malenka ever since and actively engaged in politics," explained Senga.

Sanagu raised the lamp to examine him more closely.
He was tall and fair in complexion, with strands of hair

hanging on his chin in parchments as if somebody had deliberately planted them there. The room was not hot but sweat ran down his arms and his shirt showed dampness on the sleeves and the sides. He sat up straight in the chair like a student in a classroom in front of a strict teacher. His handkerchief could not do the job of mopping his face and arms properly because it was completely soaked.

"I have come to see you because I want the political seat in Malenka North," he said with his eyes fixed on him. He searched his pocket and brought out the sum of one hundred thousand Leones.

"Please tell me whether my chances would good or not", he said, handing over the money to him.

Sanagu received the money and put it away. He got up, opened a bag and brought out a purse. In that purse, there were a handful of cowries and a white piece of cloth. The cloth was neatly spread on the floor mat to receive the cowries which were well shaken in a small calabash dish. He then studied the permutations and combinations of the cowries on the mat. He picked each cowry with words which could not be understood. He went through the process four times and then drew the attention of Senga to the final combinations.

"You see these two cowries", pointing his finger at them,

"They represent your chances. They have occurred three times together, meaning that your chances are very good," he said, emphasizing the words "very good" repeatedly.

Senga's smiles broadened and the sweat from his head continued its downward pour on his face. He used both his hands to wipe his face but they were not effective. He then squeezed dry his soaked handkerchief in one corner of the room and then mopped his face and head dry. The little joy that brightened his visage was short lived when he made another pronouncement.

"You see this single cowry," pressing his finger firmly on it. "This is the obstacle to your ambition and it is indeed a big obstacle," he told him in a firm tone.

A few minutes elapsed before he found the words to speak.

"Is the obstacle insurmountable?" he asked, anxious for a quick, positive answer.

"No, but everything will depend mainly on your moral strength. Truly, the single cowry represents a sacrifice. In fact, a superior sacrifice in order to get the position that you have asked for", he Said.

"What is a superior sacrifice? Do you mean a cow?" Senga asked trying to get to the bottom of the matter quickly.

He smiled and shook his head in the negative.

"A cow is by no means a superior sacrifice. Please go and find out for yourself", he advised and escorted him to the door and bid him farewell.

As Senga stepped out on the street, the idea of the superior sacrifice occupied his mind immediately.

"If a cow is not a superior sacrifice what else could it be?" he said to himself. "In the normal sense a cow is superior to sheep, goat, and chickens. What else is superior to a cow?" he pondered as he walked right across the street to where he had parked his Motorbike. He arrived home very late that night.

"Kola, Kola, for good price," shouted Benakie on the

streets of Madina. He slept there to contact Kola dealers early in the morning before they went to their farms. Overnight he bought nearly a sack full which he kept in Brima's house. By mid-day, he had bought an additional quantity which he sorted out in sizes and kept them in different sacks.

Benakie was a rice farmer many years ago but lately his farms failed him for two consecutive years; in the first year he planted his seeds according to the normal farming calendar but the rains fell very late and the seeds did not germinate, and in the second year the rains fell early but far in excess and destroyed some seeds. During those years life became so difficult for him that he sold off all the rice he had kept for replanting and used the money to trade in kola nuts.

The trade proved promising and the fear of returning to rice farming again was already out of his mind because he was making reasonable profits and his family was not sleeping on empty stomach.

However, the main challenge of the trade was moving from place to place on foot and buying whatever quantities were available. In some villages, he got not more than one tenth of 50kg sack, but in some others he got enough to carry. Another tedious aspect of the job was carrying the load on his head where the routes were not motorable. The new trade made him known in many villages and towns. One day he was in Madina and the next he would be either in Kambaya or Fitia, depending on where news was good about the Kola trade. Within one week he passed through Madina, Fitia and Seneun, sleeping where he had more business and more loads. Sometimes he had more than one sack to carry and in such situations, he would either pay somebody or ask a friend to carry his extra load.

His final destination was Malenka where he sold his goods to business men from various parts of the country.

In Malenka, he lived in a house which had a big bedroom and a cubicle for his Kola nuts and other minor items that appealed to him for business. Once in Malenka, he was sure that his goods would be sold without much delay. Once he had the money in his pockets, he almost forgot the bumpy, long distances and heavy loads that he had to cope with. For him, all of that was history as he was much more concerned with his worth at the end of his transactions. Kola trade had proved good and nothing was going to bring him back to rice farming.

Back in Malenka, Senga's mind was fully occupied with the issue of the sacrifice. He could not sleep properly due to the threat that the sacrifice posed to his ambition. But he was still hopeful because he was told that the obstacle was surmountable. He was therefore prepared to do whatever it takes to secure the sacrifice. But he was still doubtful over what Sanagu meant by a superior sacrifice. A sacrifice that was superior to a cow remained a critical issue in his mind.

He reflected on his tradition and customs and found no evidence that an untamed animal was offered as a sacrifice. He therefore ruled out the untamed animal kingdom as far as animal sacrifice was concerned. He then looked at the issue logically by agreeing that only human beings were superior to animals and therefore a superior sacrifice meant a human sacrifice. By arriving at that conclusion a strange feeling of fear ran through his spine and sweat covered his body. He closed his eyes to force a sleep but he could not. He turned left and then right but no sleep came to his eyes. He laid awake with his eyes moving from one object to another without any particular interest. While he counted the sticks that made up the ceiling, his mind concentrated only on one thing, the human sacrifice that stood as an obstacle to his ambition.

"Why is the sacrifice preventing me from having power, wealth and fame?" he pondered.

He convinced himself that Sanagu meant a human sacrifice but wanted him to figure it out for himself. The more he thought of that type of sacrifice, the more sleeplessness gripped his eyes and the more he sweated on his bed. At the first cock crow he got out of bed looking very weak. He walked to the nearby stream and immersed himself completely in it. He washed properly and walked back to town feeling refreshed.

Kaimoto stood directly behind Tenja who sat on a low bench and dished out food in bowls.

"Who is behind me?" She asked without looking back. "Can I help you?" She asked again.

"I am a visitor and I am hungry," said Kaimoto, distorting his voice to conceal his identity. But Tenja knew his voice very well.

"If you had slept in Seneun you would have found an empty house," She said very convinced that the voice was that of Kaimoto.

He stepped out in front of her and she looked up and gave him a broad smile. As they ate their dinner together, he brought out of his hand bag some items including a beautiful necklace and handed them over to her. She gave him another broad smile and thanked him.

As both of them continued with their meal, Tenja had

a few questions to ask but she was not convinced it was the appropriate time to ask questions. She wanted to know how he got the money that he used to purchase the items. There was no doubt that she appreciated them very much and was convinced that he loved her. As far as she remembered, he went with an empty hand bag and had no money to the best of her knowledge.

Why was he not telling her the truth about his income? She pondered.

He realized that Tenja was thinking hard and then he shook her on the shoulder.

"What are you thinking about?" he inquired jokingly

"Nothing," She said

"There is something on your mind, but let us get inside", he said convincingly. Both of them got up and went into their bedroom.

"What is it Tenja? Tell me what is wrong? He insisted.

"Well, you brought items without telling me how you got the money. This is my concern.

Does it make sense to you?" she asked staring directly at him

"You are right, but there is nothing sinister in the whole affair," he said and explained how Sanagu had asked him for parts of a chimpanzee which he needed urgently. When he killed the chimpanzee that was found in the mango tree, he removed those parts and took them to him. It was on account of the parts that he gave him one hundred thousand Leones.

"Good, I am happy because I now know the source of your income. Thank you very much", she concluded and jumped on the bed.

Panga had no time to rest. The moment she put down

her load from the trip and greeted her father and neighbors, she went out to meet her friends. Although she made two friends in Baudu, she was always happy with her friends in Madina. She was fond of Mina and wanted to be in her company at all times because she was full of interesting stories.

Mina was thin and slightly taller than Panga but when they wrestled Panga brought her down most times.

They loved each other and nothing ever separated them. When Mina had a quarrel with other children, the parents would not allow Panga to serve as a witness and vice versa because they found no fault in each other. They were together for just a short time when a little girl came running towards them. Panga got up immediately because she knew that the little girl was sent by her mother to call her. She got the message right because the little girl said it exactly.

"See you in the evening" said Mina as she ran towards her house.

Senga lost weight and that was noticeable even by his wife and children immediately they arrived in Malenka. They asked him whether he was sick but he told them he was quite OK. The children were attending school in Duma and their mother stayed there to give them both financial and moral support. At the end of each school term, she brought them home to see relatives and to relax. Before schools reopened, she gathered enough rice and other essential food items which she took along with her.

Saley was a middle aged woman with twins, Fenda and Kenda, the only children she had. She loved them because she got them when most people felt she would no longer bear children as she was considered a barren woman. She knew about the gossip but she prayed to her maker to change her situation and indeed her prayers were answered with twins.

Senga made sure she took the children back to Duma earlier than usual. He was ashamed of what he looked like. Often the children found him lost in his thoughts and he could not tell them what was wrong. They knew that something was wrong somewhere but he tried as much as possible to avoid them. Once the children were back in Duma, the joy of rejoining their friends in school made them forget entirely about what happened to their father.

Any time Senga was alone the issue of the human sacrifice came alive in his mind. It was such a tormenting feeling that he tried but could not get rid of it. It reminded him that power, wealth and fame would not come unless and until the sacrifice was accomplished and that time was running out. He was under tremendous pressure as general elections got closer.

Finally he made up his mind to see Sanagu once more and to say that he understood what a superior sacrifice was and that he was prepared for it no matter what the consequences would be. He felt that it was his turn to enjoy political power and nothing was going to stop him. He recalled that he had campaigned for many candidates in the same constituency but there was nothing to show for his hard work. He was quite convinced that it was his turn and that he should be nominated for the forthcoming elections.

It was very late in the evening that he took his handbag and rode his Motorbike towards Seneun through Fitia.

23

He arrived there very late. He parked his Motorbike by the side of the house and walked into the verandah. He tapped on the door twice.

The door opened slowly and a flash light shone on his face.

"Good day", said Indy.

"Come right in," she said removing the rays of light from him. He walked into the house and waited patiently for Indy to announce him. He walked right into Sanagu's bedroom when Indy said it was OK.

He sat in the chair by the door after shaking hands with him.

"So you have come back?" asked Sanagu.

"Yes, I am back and to say that I have understood what a superior sacrifice is," he said and paused for a moment and then continued.

"I am prepared to secure the sacrifice despite the consequences. You have told me already that my chance of success was good and I am not prepared to throw it away", he said with desperation in his voice.

The moment he pronounced these words he was a changed man.

He was no longer the timid type but bold and fearless. He spoke with confidence and determination as if he had absolute control over the events that would come into play.

"Where is the sacrifice?" he asked to press him further to the goal.

"I will bring it if I know exactly what I am supposed to do when I get it," he said without mincing his words.

"You need a female, preferably a virgin. You need the skin on the palms and the private parts and some of her blood. In the case of a virgin, you must deflower her after which you can then go ahead to get the required parts. Try as much as possible not to involve more than three people in the deal and ensure that the associates are absolutely under your control. The deal must be a secret for life and none of them should be allowed to betray you. If anyone leaks the secret it is quite clear that you will not live. Therefore anyone who has a potential to betray you must not be allowed to live," he elaborated.

"On the question of fees, I need three cows or its equivalent in Leones. One cow before the sacrifice and two afterwards", he concluded and bid him farewell.

He got up and put his hand in his pocket and brought out a neatly packed sum of one hundred thousand Leone notes and put it on the mat where Sanagu sat and then walked out of the room through the parlor into the verandah.

He crossed the gaping gutter in front of the house and walked to his Motorbike. He sat on it and rode back to Malenka through the harmattan winds that made him shiver throughout the journey.

The evening brought the children together under Mina's roof as usual. Panga had already taken her seat right beside her.

"Once upon a time", Mina began in a cool and calculated voice. "The fortune teller of the rat kingdom told the rats that the era of the cat kingdom was at its end. He said that the last cat will die and will be discovered by a rat any moment in the near future. The rats jubilated and waited patiently for that day that will give them absolute freedom of movement, freedom of speech and association and the freedom to own the land which was their bona fide property. They argued that their great, great grandfather leopard rat was the one who first lived in the land. But the cats argued that leopard rat lived in the land but that it grew up in a cat skin.

The rats agreed that leopard rat indeed grew up in a cat skin but that the skin was either brought from another continent or the cat wandered into the land and died due to climatic conditions. There was no end to these contestations. But one day a rat was looking for food in a dust bin and then discovered a dead cat. He ran to the elders and told them what he had seen. Within a short time the rats assembled to discuss the issue in relation to the prophecy. It was unanimously agreed by the rats that the dead cat was the prophecy. For confirmation, a team of experts made of old rats who were familiar with the cat kingdom were allowed to examine the cat to prove the cause of death.

The dead cat was then brought out from a highly secured hideout and examined. It was discovered that pieces of raw meat were in its claws which symbolized that it hunted a few days ago. No bones were broken and the eyes were intact. His general outlook was good and showed a sign of good living. The stomach was opened and the intestines were in order and showed no signs of rupture. The contents of the intestines and other organs were examined. There was no poisonous weed, herb or meat found. The cause of death was unknown as far as the examination went. The team therefore concluded that the cause of death was beyond their understanding."
Mina narrated.

She paused and asked for some water. One of the children, captivated by the story, ran into the house quickly and brought a cup of water for her. She drank a mouthful and looked around her and saw anxiety on the faces of the children. Then she continued the narrative.

"The team and the elders met and discussed and concluded that the death of the cat was in line with the prophecy. They therefore appointed a day and a place for all rats to assemble and to demonstrate their freedom," she paused again and raised the wick of the lamp so that she could see the children around her clearly.

"The rats gathered and indeed it was a big gathering of all types of rats. They formed a long queue with the big and old rats at the rear. The musicians with their drums and flutes were right in the middle of the queue.

Then a big rat climbed a tree nearby where all the rats could see him and shouted for the attention of all and announced:

"We are free indeed and we are here to jubilate. We will match through the town, down to the river and back. The cat kingdom has ended", he said and descended quickly, continued Mina.

Then the flutes and drums blasted music into the air. Ray, Ray, the cat is no more

- No more
- No more

Ray, Ray, Nyangumeh San-nyo

- San-nyo
- San-nyo

Ray, Ray, Nyangumaan M'banda

- Mbanda
- M'banda,"

It was indeed amazing to see big and small rats matching forward to the sound of the flutes and drums and repeating the sounds, no more, no more, San -nyo, San-nyo, M'banda, M'banda. It was indeed a long queue from one end of the town right to the center. The rats

27

were jubilant and fearless and believed strongly that the prophecy was correct.

As the rear of the Matchers got into the middle of the town, the cats were amazed and taken aback by the demonstration. They organized themselves quickly into two groups. There was the advance group which went ahead of the demonstrators using shortcuts while the other group watched the rear.

Then suddenly, a deafening sound of a cat was heard that halted the match instantaneously. And within a split second the cats encircled all of them and the sound of twi, Twi was heard all over the place. The rats died by their thousands but still some of them escaped. The cats were poised to bring to justice anyone who demonstrated, and up to this day they are looking for the demonstrators", said Mina.

So, the fortune teller was a liar? Panga asked.

"Yes, he was a big liar," said Mina.

The children were very happy indeed and sang the song, no more, no more, San-nyo, San-nyo M'banda, M'banda as they went away to their various houses.

Senga woke up in the morning wondering who would be his helpers.

He recalled that Sanagu had told him that the number must not exceed three and none of them should be allowed under any circumstance to leak the secret.

He thought about the issue for a long time and some possible names came to his mind which he analyzed over and over. Definitely, he could not go far with some of the names because he felt they would not be characters strong enough to keep the secret for life. However, he kept two names, Abu and Kpaku after a comprehensive assessment. He was confident that those two would keep whatever secret he shared with them.

Abu became a businessman when he called off schooling due to an illness which occurred whenever he had examinations. He was moved to various schools in many towns but the illness and its untimely occurrence continued everywhere he went.

At the end he left school and had enough justification for leaving. He therefore did not bow his head in shame even among his colleagues who had proceeded to higher levels of learning. He was bold to tell people that his performance in school was better than some colleagues who continued their schooling and eventually succeeded.

Some of his colleagues did not remember him well enough because he dropped off from school too early but he would be the one to remind them of the days they were all in school.

With a series of broken marriages he lived alone in a cubicle of a house he constructed by himself. At some point in the construction process, the foundation shifted and so was the house, giving it a leaning posture. It was commonly referred to as the leaning house of Malenka. Sometimes he told his audience who criticized the awkward structure that he had planned it that way. Many believed that one day it would collapse.

He was alone in the house for most of the time because some people were afraid to lodge in it for obvious reasons. Despite the negative public opinion he lived in his house and without fear.

Although Senga had already decided who would be his helpers, he still found it difficult to approach them on the issue. Twice he had booked appointments with Abu but canceled them even before the time. Some fear was restraining him from letting somebody into the secret that early. He tried to combat that fear but it kept coming back and that delayed his meeting with Abu. But one day he made up his mind and took Abu on his Motorbike and rode to a place far away from the town. And when he was sure that they were alone he explained to him in great detail all that concerned the sacrifice.

Abu listened carefully, nodding his head on some familiar points.

At the end of his long speech, he was expecting him to make a comment immediately. But he remained silent with his face fixed in one direction as if he had seen a strange thing there.

He waited but no comments came. Then he became a bit uncomfortable with his friend's unusual silence. Could it be that he was already afraid? He kept asking himself without attempting to cause him to speak up.

Abu looked round about them and then finally asked.

"Who is the sacrifice?"

He smiled and got up once more and told him that the sacrifice was the assignment for both of them. Abu had still not said much and that was still worrying him.

Was it the taking of human life that kept him cold? What was it that made him behave so differently? Could it have been the pay or benefit that was not mentioned? He kept on asking himself.

Then he realized that he needed to explain to him that the reward would be to crown him the town chief of Malenka and to supervise the collection of local taxes, market dues and the proceeds of all court cases. And suddenly Abu's face lit up. He cleared his throat and told him that such an operation was most likely feasible in

Duma.

"Why in Duma?" He asked with a certain amount of curiosity in his voice.

"In Duma you have prostitutes and street children who can be trapped very easily. Once there is money we can take them wherever we want", he said his face beaming with light.

Senga shook his head in agreement.

He was happy at last that his friend was fully on board and showed determination to address the issue of the sacrifice. The two men sat down for many hours discussing the details of the actions required. They finally agreed on Duma and itemized the instruments required, the date and the amount that was needed. It was a sensational meeting that ended without much controversy.

The next day Abu and Senga boarded a vehicle to Duma. They were well prepared to secure the sacrifice. They had special knives, blades, hooks and sacks. They also bought enough assorted drinks and were quite determined to secure the sacrifice, no matter what it may cost them.

When they arrived in Duma, they went to Senga's family where he explained to his wife that he was on an assignment. When it was nightfall he drove the taxi cab towards the city Centre, not in search of additional income for his family but in search of a sacrifice which was an obstacle to his political ambition.

He drove and stopped at various points in the city and drove towards the western region and located a guest house at the extreme end of the city. He paid for rooms 10 and 11, settled there for a brief moment and then drove back to the city centre to a spot known as Sparks.

At Sparks the lighting system was not very good but people still found their way in and out of the long one flat building which had many partitions and many youthful occupants and visitors. The smell of cannabis was so strong around the building as if somebody was smoking it close by. The building stood on a slope a few meters away from the street.

As they moved closer to the building, a lady met them and asked if they were there for business but they lied that they were looking for somebody and moved ahead. The next moment another asked them the same question and indicated that she was available. After negotiating the price per night with her, all three of them moved towards the vehicle and boarded it. She sat in the back seat with Abu and Senga sped off with them. The car arrived at the guest house and Senga spoke to the security personnel of the guest house to allow him to park the car in such a way that it could move out easily without any other vehicles blocking it. That request was granted and the vehicle was parked close to the out gate.

The three of them moved into room 10 and occupied it temporarily. The lady sat on one of the available chairs in the room whilst Senga and Abu scuttled between room 10 and the car, bringing in hand bags, a carton of star beer, a carton of stout and a big bottle of vodka.

A table was set and a mini party began in room 10.

The diminutive lady was neatly dressed with thick black hair flowing from the back of her head to her back.

It was far from being her natural hair but it was so well attached that one hardly knew the difference. She told the two men that she did not operate on names but for convenience she should be referred to as Beauty.

After one or two pints of beer each, the two men got up and explained to her that they were going into room 11 to settle some issues and left her alone to help herself with the drinks. She smiled when she realized that she was in control of everything. She engaged the bottles because she was not sure the opportunity would remain to be the same, because the two men may eventually decide otherwise, renege on the contract and the opportunity to continue drinking would be lost immediately. She made up her mind to drink as much as she could in their absence.

As she drank and began to feel tipsy, her mind went to the bags and money. She got up, went out briefly and realized that the two men were still busy discussing. She came into the room again and tried to open one of the bags.

Her index finger came against a sharp object. Immediately blood oozed out of the minor cut on the finger .She closed the bag and put her handkerchief on the cut and held it tightly with her left hand to prevent blood spilling on the floor. She went out and walked across the street to a nearby shop and got a medicated plaster for the finger. She plastered the cut, got back to the room and continued drinking the different types of the available drinks.

The two men later joined her and apologized for their long absence.

She was almost drunk but continued drinking different combinations of wine. By mid-night, she was dead drunk and unable to uphold herself. She staggered to the bed and lay on her back, and within seconds she was fast asleep.

Abu forced some more beer down her throat and then took her to the bathroom and laid her on the sponge brought for the purpose. He forced some more vodka into her mouth and then tied her hands behind her back and put a basin close to her neck.

When he was sure that she was completely helpless he took a sharp knife and pressed the sharpest edge against her arm but she did not move or shout. She lay still, almost in an unconscious state, and snored at intervals. He made a concoction of beer and vodka and forced it down her throat again and waited to see how she reacted. She tried to throw up but she could not.

Meanwhile Senga was busy tying her feet together and keeping watch. For most of the time he was close to the door listening for the least noise. Once or twice a client walked past room 10 and Senga signaled to Abu to hold on.

Later, the lady at the front desk of the guest house noticed blood on the floor. She took a piece of cloth from her drawer, put some water on it and went to the spot to clean it off. Before she finished cleaning it, she noticed another spot. She realized that the problem was bigger than she thought. She went back to her seat and took an empty bucket and some water and followed the spots of blood along the corridor.

Apparently, Beauty was unconscious but she reacted sharply when a piece of cloth was put on her mouth. She turned and kicked, not robustly as she was very weak. Abu took the knife and made a sign to him that it was time. He held her throat firmly and brought the knife against it.

But suddenly there was a knock on the door by the lady at the front desk when she heard scuffles in room 10 after cleaning the blood spot by the door.

She knocked on the door again to know what was happening inside. Then, a man's face appeared and explained that they had a problem with a lady who was drunk.

She told them that they were disturbing other clients and promised to keep an eye on them. She stood there for some time until there was no more noise coming from the room. She strolled back to the front desk still contemplating on what may have happened. The drops of blood leading to the room and the strange noises from inside occupied her mind.

Abu had removed the ropes from her hands and feet, hid all the instruments and put her back on the bed.

The front desk lady came back and knocked on room 10 and waited but there was no answer.

"I noticed drops of blood right up to your room. Was there any accident?" she asked, looking very suspicious.

"No, we are all ok, no accident," Senga hurriedly told the lady who looked on unconvinced.

"Anyway, we will shall look into that in the morning," said the lady as she moved back to the front desk

Abu was busy pouring water on Beauty to revive her. After much work she opened her eyes and looked on sheepishly as Abu poured more water on her head and some milk into her throat from time to time.

Very early the next morning she was able to stand up and barely managed to walk without help. Senga paid her and let her leave the room without much delay.

She walked past the front desk unnoticed and stopped a Motorbike which sped off with her along the street with less traffic.

Back into the car the two men drove off in complete silence.

They were tired and discouraged. They spent most of the day sleeping at home with Senga's family.

Saley got lunch ready by mid-day and woke them up. They ate and sat around for some time and discussed what more to do in the coming hours.

By nightfall they had their bath, dressed up and drove off to the city center again. They parked the car by a big abandoned building along the street. With the help of search lights they went into the building which was completely dark.. As the search lights penetrated the various corners of the building there was an unusual movement of people away from the lights. Finally, the lights rested on the face of a teenage boy.

"I am not a criminal. I don't have a place to sleep that is why I am here", said the boy crying and begging for mercy.

"Please don't take me to the Police station", he begged, moving towards the two men.

Abu then told him that they were not police men and that they were there looking for a girl that absconded from home a few days ago.

The boy's face lit up with joy. He thought he was already in police hands for petty crimes he may not have committed.

"What is the girl's name"? The boy asked them.

"Don't worry about the name, we know her and when we see her we can identify her without any difficulty", Senga said authoritatively.

The boy beckoned to them and the two men followed him. He led them through a back opening without a door into a smaller house a few meters away. He took them to a room on the left wing of the house. The inmates of that room were all asleep on a long mat across the room. They woke up with a start as the beam of the search lights fell on them. They were teenage street girls.

They got up and retreated to one corner in a cluster and waited to know who those men were. As they waited they mumbled words like "The police", "rapists", and "thieves" to each other.

"We are neither the police, nor rapists or thieves", said Abu.

"We are here looking for a young girl that absconded from home a few days ago. If you can allow us to see all of you, then that will be the end of our mission", continued Abu.

The children then broke the cluster and came forward. Abu and Senga examined them as they appeared under the beam of the two bright search lights. The examination continued as more of the children came out from various rooms of the small house.

The beam then fell on one that attracted the attention of the two men.

She was tall and dark, in an oversized dress which was torn across the chest partially showing her breasts. She moved quickly away from the light and stood aside.

After the exercise Senga announced to the children that the girl they were looking for was not among them. He put his hand deep into his bag and brought out two packets of biscuits and some money which he handed over to them. While the children were busy discussing the method of sharing the money and biscuits, Abu beckoned on the tall girl and asked her if she would be willing to help them find the missing girl.

The girl thought over it for a moment and responded.

"But I don't know her", she said.

"We shall bring her photo tomorrow. Where can we locate you in the morning?" asked Abu in a soft voice.

"There is a tree outside the big building along the street. I shall be under the shade of that tree in the morning" said the girl and moved quickly and joined the others for her own share of the biscuits and money.

The boy led the two men through another route to the street where the car was parked and went back to his hideout with a few Leones in his pocket from his benefactors.

The two men were quite satisfied with what they had achieved over night. They discussed all that was necessary relating to their mission as they drove back home.

The next day they got up early and took their breakfast rather hastily. Senga gave some money to his wife and got her permission to take the car back to Malenka because he was on an important assignment. He promised that within two days the car would be returned. He then bid his children farewell and assured them that he loved them.

They boarded the car and sped across the tarmac towards the city center. The little dark, tall girl kept herself reminded about the appointment with the two men who visited them the previous night. She wondered why somebody that was fed, lodged and well taken care of would abandon such opportunities to come to the type of life she lived. She could not understand such behaviour because it violated common sense. She convinced herself that such a thing was possible only where food, lodge and care were absent in a home.

She always stood aside and admired parents who bought biscuits for their children and held their hands to ensure that they were safe across the streets. She longed for parental care of any kind to remove her from the streets. She could not remember seeing her parents. She was told that her parents died in the war. She felt bitter that the war was so wicked to have taken both her parents at the same time.

An inmate just rushed into the room and broke her chain of thought. She kept the appointment in mind and did not allow any distractions. She reminded herself of the appointment very often throughout the night.

The next day she got up early and put on her day dress and got ready to meet the two men. She was anxious to receive the photo of the girl that absconded from home. She was determined to see that girl and to find out why she left home. She would visit all the sites where street children gather just to find her. Her curiosity grew as she walked to the tree where the men promised to meet her.

The two men arrived at the big building, parked their car along the street and walked to the tree. They found her waiting for them.

"Are you the one we spoke to last night?" asked Abu, smiling.

"Yes", said the girl.

"What is your name?" asked Senga, holding her by her hand. "My friends call me Tally," replied the girl laughing.

Senga opened his bag and took out a photograph of a young girl and presented it to Tally. She examined the photo closely but could not remember meeting that face anywhere. She examined it again and shook her head to signify that she had never met her before.

"Can you help us locate her?" asked Senga, apologetically.

"Take me to a place called Punk, which is not too far away", said Tally.

Senga then moved to the car followed by Abu and Tally. The three boarded the car and Senga drove in the direction provided by Tally.

A few minutes later, Tally looked out and asked him to stop. She asked them to wait in the car while she went across the road and entered a house a few meters away from the street.

She came out of the house after a brief moment, holding the photo in her right hand and crossed the street to where the car was parked.

"She is not here", said Tally, holding out the photo to Senga."Thank you very much", said Senga, taking the photo from her.

Abu opened the car and asked her to come in so that they could drop her by the big building, an offer which she accepted without any hesitation.

On board the car, Abu turned to her and asked her what plans she had for the future? Without wasting any time Tally told him that she was looking for parental care and love. She told them that living on the streets was risky and difficult and there was no one to turn to in the days of adversity. She explained further that their lodging houses changed from time to time due to raids by unknown persons, thieves and police men.

"Do you mind if we take you from the streets and make your life good in a respectful home?" Abu asked, showing some interest.

"I don't mind", she replied "But who will take care of me?" she inquired anxiously.

"My wife" said Senga.

"Where does she live?" she inquired again.

"She lives at 13 Lower Papas Street," said Senga.

The address rang a bell in her mind. She recalled that she was on that street some time ago looking for a cleaning job. She recalled too that she washed dishes out there and at the end she had some food and some coins. She remembered the street very well and the lady who offered her the cleaning job.

The car stopped at the big house.

"We are prepared to take you right away to make your life good at home", said Abu smiling.

"Are you prepared to come with us now?" Asked Senga.

"As long as your wife is going to look after me I am prepared. Just allow me a few minutes to take my hand bag" she said trying to get out of the car. She came out and went through the sidewalks to the back of the big building.

The two men waited anxiously, noting every second of her stay. They could not hide their anxiety. Once in a while they opened the doors, came out, looked around and got back into the car. They thought they had found a solution to their problem and nothing on earth would make them lose out. They kept looking in the direction of the big building hoping to see Tally.

At a point in time Abu felt that Tally had overstayed and came out of the car and walked half way through the distance and stopped and returned. He could not find the words to use in case he found a clever and mature person with her. They could not even discuss any other issue because if Tally did not return then all their time and efforts would have gone in vain.

Suddenly, Tally appeared with three girls that stood on the side of the street and watched her walk to the car.

The looks on the faces of the girls were mixed. One looked happy and smiled as Tally went away from them but the other two looked somber and unhappy. Whatever reason may have caused them to feel the way they did, Tally had left them and they could do nothing about it. They watched her until she entered the car which moved away slowly until it disappeared completely from sight.

Tally was happy but did not show that on her face. She felt she had completely escaped the life of fear and uncertainty and was going to be in a home where she was going to be protected and fed. She was no longer going to request for work for her survival or spend a lot of time protecting the little she had from inmates. She felt too that she had escaped street brutality and police interrogations, which sometimes landed her into prison.

The worst she feared was rapists among their colleague males and others who went desperately in search of the girl child. She recalled she had to run for hours to escape a man who was drunk and fearlessly chased her from place to place late at night.

As she reflected on her past difficult life, she lost contact with the reality around her. She looked up and realised that Senga was speeding and she noticed that they had gone far into the city without arriving at 13 Lower Papas Street where she was going to stay.

She looked out and realized too that they were on the main street that cut across the city. She waited patiently to see whether he would take a left or right turn to usher them to Papas street. But unfortunately, he drove continuously along the main street and was still speeding. The traffic on the main street was not heavy but once in a while he had to slow down the car to allow pedestrians to use the Zebra and then moved faster again within a few minutes.

It was during those temporary stops that Tally had the opportunity to look out of the car to view the area to see whether it had any resemblance to Papas Street which she knew well enough. What she saw each time was different but she was hopeful that they would arrive there sometime. After all, she consoled herself that she was not familiar with most of the streets in the city and therefore would not know which street led to which. She sat back and tried to control her emotions but her curiosity grew more and more. So many questions came to her mind at the same time: why was he speeding? Why have they stopped talking to me? Why are they talking to themselves in low tones? She could not provide answers to all of these questions but had faith in the promise to remove her from the streets. She could not believe that those two men were liars. They looked good and apparently gentle. Why would they lie to a little girl worth nothing? She pondered.

He accelerated the car as if he was in a competition, focusing only on the gear, the steering and accelerator and nothing else. The car surged forward and raced through the hot air leaving behind it a thick black smoke.

It became crystal clear to Tally that the two men were up to something. The speed and the silence made her feel trapped. She thought she had made a mistake by allowing herself to come that far. She was quite convinced that she was in big trouble. She had two options; jumping out of the car, but the high speed would send her crashing dead on the ground, and crying aloud so that the passers-by would hear and intervene. But the car was speeding so fast that the noise of the winds crashing against the windscreen would swallow her little voice and render the venture ineffective.

She looked outside the car again and realized that they were outside of the city as she could see tall trees in the bush along the road.

"What do these men want? Is it sex or is it my life?"

She asked herself repeatedly. She sweated and felt bitterness on her tongue as if she had swallowed a bitter pill. Her whole body became cold and she shivered. Tears ran down her eyes caused by the wind that came directly against her face through a lowered window glass where she peeped almost continuously. She wiped away the tears with the back of her hand from time to time.

As the car approached the cross roads, a traffic warden flagged it down and asked the driver to park the car on the side of the road. The warden came closer to the car and examined the tires and then asked for his driver's license which he produced quickly and handed it over to him.

The warden examined it briefly and boarded the car.

"Drive off to the Police station", said the warden", pointing at the route to the station.

"But my driver's license is up to date", he said

"Move", said the warden.

He moved the car towards the Police station which was about 300 meters away from the cross-roads.

On arrival he parked the car on the side of the station building and followed the warden into the charging room. He was told he had committed five traffic offences including over speeding, smooth tires, broken headlights, and an expired vehicle license and Insurance. He was denied self-bail and temporarily detained.

With the warden at his back he beckoned on Abu to come to the station.

Abu, in a panicky mood came out of the car and walked right into the station where he was asked to wait. While he waited his whole attention was on Tally and the possibility of losing her.

"Will she wait or run away?" he pondered.

Tally opened the car, looked around and walked away with her bag tucked under her arm. She ran quickly towards the cross-roads. Within a short time she arrived there, weary and panting for breath. The next moment a bus arrived with the driver's mate standing at the door of the bus and shouting Duma, Duma, to draw the attention of waiting passengers to his vehicle.

Tally seized the opportunity and ran to the bus which parked a few meters away from her. The driver's mate opened the bus and allowed her inside and the bus took off immediately.

The two men came out of the Police station and ran to the car. Tally was absent and she could not be found around the police station. Senga drove the car to the cross-roads but she was not there either and nobody seemed to have seen her.

"We have lost her", said Senga to Abu who could not say a word.

He drove back to 13 Papas street prepared to appear in court for the traffic offences he had committed.

The next morning he appeared in court and somehow his offences were reduced to one charge and he paid the fine and left the court house that same day.

"Kola, Kola, for good price. Sell to me now and make a good gain"

Benakie cried out, as he walked along the streets of Madina. He got more kola nuts out there than the neighboring towns. That was why he came there more often, especially in the dry season. He maintained a very good relationship with the farmers to ensure that they did not sell to other buyers. He made a gift of salt, magi cubes, and small quantities of sugar to them whenever he sold his goods in Malenka.

The farmers spoke good things about him and made sure he was favored in the face of any competition. He bought quite a substantial quantity of kola nuts in Madina every season, all of which he took to Malenka for sale. He made good profits out there, the reason why he treated the Madina farmers with seriousness. He paid them correct sums and did not owe them any amounts of money. Occasionally, he gave money to some in advance for late harvest but everything worked well for him.

In every town he kept his wares with a friend. In Madina he kept it with Brima whose quiet disposition and kindness he admired so much. One day he gave him some money in return for his moral support and kindness but he refused the money on the grounds that friendship was not a commodity for sale. He bought enough kola nuts and increased his stock with him before he left for Malenka the next day.

Senga and Abu made the journey back to Malenka late in the evening. They were discouraged about the obstructions they had in carrying out their mission in Duma. They had taken the necessary steps and items required for the operation but mishap or bad luck stood firmly in their way. Without the intervention of the lady at the front desk of the guest house and the traffic warden everything would have been OK. They decided to forget about their failures and to continue working hard towards achieving the goal.

They sat together and discussed the way forward. They looked at various options and the risks that they did not consider initially and then realized that some of the options they had chosen were not feasible and may cause information to leak out easily. They also considered individuals who could help them out without getting them into the main secret and they found the second option more appropriate.

One name that came up each time they went through the list of names they had compiled was Benakie. They knew him as a man who was very familiar with the towns and villages of the region through his kola nut trade. They therefore considered him to be the appropriate person to contact.

Chapter Three

The Search Continues

They agreed upon the instructions he needed and the amount required to getting him started. They also agreed that he should be contacted to know whether he would be available or not. At the end of the discussions, Abu strolled to his house to know whether he was at home. He knocked on his front door but there was no answer. He knocked again and heard some movements inside and waited patiently.

Then, he heard the key turn once, twice and the door opened without any face showing up. "Come in", said Benakie. He was weak and tired and not fully recovered from sleep. He walked the long distance from Madina with sacks of kola nuts. Although he had rested many times on the way, it was still a tedious journey.

Abu entered and found him sitting on his bed. Both men discussed the challenges of life generally and agreed that their fathers and grandfathers had better times with more opportunities.

He then informed him that he and Senga would like to talk to him the next day. They agreed on the time and Senga's house was the venue.

Benakie promised that he would be there on time. He was happy that the meeting came to an end quickly because he was tired and needed more sleep. He lay on his back and the next moment he was already snoring.

The next day they met at Senga's house at the stipulated time. They entered an inner room and Senga made sure nobody else was around. He closed both the front and back doors firmly to prevent any intruder into the room.

Benakie sat exactly opposite the two men and waited to hear what was so crucial in the invitation. He was calm and confident because he was not aware of anything he might have done to cost him money through the courts of law. This thought flashed through his mind while he waited patiently.

His chain of thought was suddenly broken when Senga spoke out rather sharply.

"You are quite aware that my wife stays permanently in Duma for the sake of my children's schooling. As a result I have had a lot of challenges with my feeding and social life in general. That has urged me to look for another wife to avoid some of the inconveniences. This is why I am appealing to you to look out for a second wife for me through your various connections in your field of trade", he explained.

"But there are conditions which you must strictly adhere to if you agree to help me out". Senga explained.

Benakie relaxed his mind properly because the invitation had nothing to do with a problem or an expenditure on his part.

"Firstly, my wife must not know anything about this arrangement until it is absolutely necessary. If by any means she comes to know about it prematurely, then she will blow up everything to pieces. Also, the parents and relatives of the selected girl must not know for the simple reason that they will discuss the issue with their friends, and their friends will discuss with their own friends, and so on and so forth, until what was a secret becomes a public affair and my wife may then have the opportunity to know. The parents and relatives will know about the issue when I have seen the girl and have decided that she is suitable. Also, she must come from a poor family background with no family members in the police force or any big establishments. This is simply because when a wife has well placed relatives in society she becomes uncontrollable and sometimes arrogant and I don't have a place for such a wife. Finally, she must be young girl, a virgin preferably", Senga concluded with sweat covering his forehead which he wiped away with his handkerchief.

"Will it be possible to see the girl if the parents are not in the know?" asked Benakie.

"This is part of your assignment. It is only but fair that I see who I am going to marry", said Senga conclusively.

Benakie nodded his head in agreement while Abu opened his bag quickly and brought out the sum of five hundred thousand Leones, which he counted leaf by leaf to ensure that it was the correct amount and handed it over to him.

"This is only a deposit. If you do the job according to the given conditions, you will receive more money", said Senga authoritatively.

Benakie received the money and promised to do his best. He looked at the amount in his hands and could not believe his eyes. He felt the amount was colossal for the job and according to Senga it was just a deposit. If he got the right choice, meeting all the conditions he would get more money. He reflected quickly on the conditions again and found that they were fairly reasonable. Senga must have had serious problems feeding himself in the absence of his wife from Malenka. Apparently, he was one of the few men in Malenka whose wife lived in another town but he was perfectly at peace with her. The move to secure a second wife for him may have been caused by the long separation between them. Anyway, he did not know what actually obtained but for the people of Malenka he lived without his wife and that became the talk of the town.

He understood why Senga wanted a second wife and thought it was quite appropriate for a man of his status.

Benakie got up, bid the two men farewell and walked out of the house feeling good.

As he walked towards his house his mind went back to the condition that the girl's relatives or parents should not be in the police force or any big establishments. Was he planning to maltreat the girl or was he simply afraid of powerful in-laws?

Benakie could not offer comments on those conditions because they were somehow strange. He would have loved to have powerful in-laws so that his wife would go to them for help at the time of financial difficulty. However, he had already accepted the money to do the job.

On arrival back home, he sat down and planned in his mind how he would approach any parent whose daughter was a likely candidate. He would tell them that he had a problem with somebody in Duma and would ask them if they had any relative in the police or any big establishment there. Anyone who answered yes was ruled out automatically and anyone who answered no would be a likely candidate. He felt that was all the preparation he needed as far as the conditions were concerned.

He brought out his empty 50 kg sacks and folded them neatly and put them in a carton. He was ready for his normal kola nut buying trip and of course the assignment.

Mina spotted Panga running towards the direction of their house and she stood and waited.

Panga arrived singing:

"Ray, Ray, Nyangumeh san-nyo, san-nyo, san-nyo". "Stop, stop", said Mina.

"It is forbidden by tradition to narrate stories in the day. I was told if you did you would be a very poor person in life and may not live long", continued Mina.

"Anyway, what kind of husband would you like to have?", asked Mina laughing and looking around in case there was an elderly person around, but fortunately there was none at that moment.

"I would like to have somebody nearly my height", said Panga. "You are short. Are you saying you would prefer a short man?" asked Mina laughing and showing the height of the man with her hand.

"Yes", said Panga with all seriousness.

"Do you know that in a certain country when the king wanted to stage a big dance to honor his people he would cunningly organize a meeting with all the short men in the region and when all of them were together in the meeting, policemen would suddenly appear, arrest and detain all of them until the festivities were over. That was done because short men were considered stubborn and could fight at the least provocation", Mina explained.

"What about you, what kind of husband would you like?" asked Panga anxiously.

"I would like to have a tall man", said Mina smiling and shaking her head.

"A tall man? As tall as a palm tree? Well, I may need a wine tapper's climber so that whenever I see him, I will climb him in order to shake his hand. You are not tall Mina. Imagine somebody as tall as a palm tree looking down on you; you will be a dwarf for him or rather a toy for him. Mina, I hope you don't mean what you are saying", said Panga with emphasis.

An elderly man stood behind Mina and tried to understand what was going on. The two girls changed the subject automatically.

"Has your father selected the site for his new rice farm for this year?" asked Mina, ignoring the person behind her.

"What has that got to do with you?" asked Panga.

"A question cannot provide an answer to another question. Answer the question and I will tell you my concern", said Mina.

"No, he has not selected the site yet", said Panga, eager to know Mina's concern.

"Imagine if our parents selected sites along the same route and not far away from each other, don't you think we shall be together for most of the time?" suggested Mina.

"Oh yes, we could have quality time to ourselves in the mornings and in the evenings when we walk along the route alone without our parents", agreed Panga excitedly.

The man behind Mina moved, leaving a trail of cigarette smoke and then disappeared into one of the houses adjacent to Mina's. Mina looked again to make sure nobody was around.

"When are you due for initiation?" She asked looking around her again.

"I believe it is this year because my parents had a good harvest last year", said Panga with a bit of hesitation in her voice.

"What about you?"She asked

"I am here only for the initiation. I need to go back to continue my schooling", Mina explained still looking around her as if somebody was eavesdropping.

"What do you know about it?" asked Panga hoping to get some information beforehand.

"I don't know anything about it, except that when my brother came out of the initiation bush he wrote a poem about his experience and gave it to me when he got wind of my coming for a similar thing. He warned me to tear the paper after reading it, but I have kept it under my clothes in my suitcase". Mina Said.

"What is a poem?" asked Panga.

"It is a piece of writing using beautiful or unusual language arranged in fixed lines that have a particular beat and often rhyme. Wait, let me bring it", said Mina and she ran across to her room and within a few minutes she came back and sat closer to Panga than before.

She produced a single paper on which was the poem. She read the poem and tried to explain it as best as she could.

"It is called "Our Beloved Children". We are children and so it is talking about us. Do you agree?" asked Mina.

Panga nodded her head in agreement.

"And it reads thus", continued Mina.

Our Beloved Children

Our beloved children
Walk the path of secret
society, Like the path of fire.

Tradition to honor with blood and
pain The repeated bites of the blade.

Like the bites of the Tsetse fly
Joyfully administered by the
initiator, To the overpowered child.
On the mat of the theatre
Blood, blood, everywhere.

The gateway to manhood, womanhood? And
boom, boom, sounds the hidden drums,
Jamming the sounds of weeping and wailing,
The secret of manhood, womanhood?

Weep not child,
Tradition good?
Found it our forefathers,
Cherished it beyond reason
And out in town,
The drummers drum,
The dancers dance,
Thrilling the day,
And undoing the night with joy.
Food, drinks everywhere
The congregation of dancers to feed.

Tradition good?

Visible and invisible scars,

The pride of membership to the survivors.

After reading the poem through, she told Panga that five words caught her attention. She then read out the words, Overpowered, blade, blood, pain and weeping.

"These five words tell me that the journey ahead of us is a difficult one altogether", said Mina.

"What journey are you talking about?" asked an elderly woman who eavesdropped.

"We are talking about the journey to my father's farm" Panga lied to hide the subject they discussed.

"What about the blade, blood and weeping that you talked about?"

The two girls kept quiet immediately.

"You better be careful you two", the elderly woman warned and walked away.

Panga got up and ran away in fear to her house.

A market day in Malenka was a day nobody would like to miss. It brought so many people together from various towns and villages across a vast region. The community leaders had erected tables and put mats on which the goods were displayed. There were various sections to the market: There was the textile section, the meat section, the agricultural tools section and a general section for agricultural products.

On a market day it was a tradition to dress up neatly and to move about in the market either to buy some items or to discover new designs in dress and foot wears. As they moved about in the market they ran into old friends or relatives from other towns that they had not seen for some time and that made the market day so important. It was also a day of making new friends and a day for petty crimes and physical confrontations when the interests of the youths clashed.

Kpaku was in the agricultural product section selling a huge pile of yams. He had sold most of it and was assured of a good evening entertainment with some of his friends. Close to the end of the day, he checked to see the total amount that he had sold. In the process of counting, he found fake currency notes amounting to over half of his sales. He was shocked and disappointed. He brought them to the attention of another friend for proper identification and indeed they were fake currencies.

He remembered the two young men who bought a large quantity of the yams. He packed the remaining yams into a sack in a hurry and kept it in a friend's store nearby and went in search of the two young men. He started in the textile market and moved through the crowd looking for them. He went round about the section but he could not see them and he left and went to the agricultural tools section and searched but they were not there either.

He returned to where he was initially and decided to move across each and every table in a section. And he walked around for so long but without any success.

He felt his efforts to plant and nurture the yams had gone in vain. He decided to keep the story to himself because it would be shameful to narrate it to anybody. He stood still to think about what next to do. And as he looked far ahead of him in one of the corners of the market, he saw the two young men moving in another direction. He recognized them by the blue dress that one of them wore and was quite convinced he was not making any mistakes in identifying them. Then he moved quickly and held them by their shirts.

"Until you pay correct amount of money for my yams, you are going nowhere", said Kpaku furiously.

The two young men tried to free themselves from his grips but they could not. They fought back by pushing, pulling and kicking at his legs.

In a feat of anger Kpaku floored both of them without much difficulty and fought desperately to maintain them in that position.

A crowd gathered immediately around them as the two men struggled to free themselves from his grips but to no avail. The market became chaotic and some items got missing from some business tables.

The market authorities came and arrested all of them but after some initial investigations, they arrested the two young men for stealing and obstructing the market's operations. The investigations proved beyond doubt that the two young men were guilty of fraud because they admitted using fake currencies to acquire the yams which they resold in the same market for a price higher than the cost price. They forfeited all the money to Kpaku and they were fined additional sums for lost items and were banned from the market for the rest of the trading season.

The news of the incidence went far and wide around the market with Kpaku's name everywhere for fishing out the two criminals from the market.

Abu and Senga met under Senga's roof to plan the way forward. They reflected on their Duma mission again which did not fail because of bad planning but simply due to mishap or bad luck. Both of them re-affirmed their commitment to the set goal and wished themselves good luck for the future mission.

They agreed between themselves that the two of them could not do the job and that they needed to recruit another person.

Senga gave Abu the opportunity to come up with a name. He sat down for quite some time selecting and cancelling names in his mind. Finally he came up with the name Kpaku.

Senga smiled broadly and nodded his head to indicate that the choice was good. He had thought about Kpaku many times whenever the need for third associate arose. The choice was good and both of them endorsed it without delay. As they were about ending their meeting there was a knock on the door.

Senga went to the front door and opened it cautiously. It was Kpaku who stood at the door.

"Come in", he said

Kpaku followed him until they came into the room.

"Did you fight?" asked Abu jokingly.

"No, I did not" he Said

"I just held the two young men in one position until the market authorities came" he continued, referring to his encounter with the thieves on the market day.

He explained in detail what had happened and they listened to him with absolute interest because they had heard different accounts of the story from different people. They felt it was their turn to know the true story.

At the end of his narrative, Abu got up and shook his hand for his courage and bravery. He told him that he could not have had the courage to go after the thieves considering the crowd that was in the market that day.

"Kpaku", said Senga quietly.

"Your father was a strong man. When rebels attacked our town many years ago he was the one who organized the young men to take up arms against them. He led the battle and fought fearlessly until the town was completely secured. The buildings standing today are due to his prowess and courage. Most other towns and villages were burnt down completely by those marauders. Your father is no more but he was my friend and both of us enjoyed our friendship throughout his life time. You are like your father both physically and in character. You are my friend too but not as close as your father was to me. Now, I want you to support me to enter parliament. If you accept you will be my campaign manager which goes with a lot of financial and material benefits and above all, the post of councilor for Malenka North will be yours. I mean what I am saying to you and I was just about sending somebody to call you when you knocked on the door. To prove to you that I am not joking," he took out the sum of two hundred and fifty thousand Leones ($50) and passed it to him through Abu.

Kpaku was overwhelmed both by what he had to say about his father and the amount that he offered. He loved his father and would not mind working closely with his friend. He promised that he would do his best and left them in a rather joyful mood. With additional money in his pockets and a prospective post of campaign manager and a future councilor for Malenka North, he felt his time to develop had come. He imagined himself addressing a large crowd of youths in a big hall. He would like to be a campaign manager in control of a vehicle with youths on board and singing the songs coined for the occasion. He hoped that he would not change his mind and give the post to somebody else. But he was confident that he would give him the post because if he had somebody else in mind he would not have spent such an amount on him for nothing. He decided to wait and see what would happen in the coming days.

"Kola, kola, for good price: Sell to me now and make a good gain", said Benakie, as he walked along the streets of Fitia.

Fitia was one of the towns that was founded about two decades ago but grew rapidly both in area and its population. Its surrounding was all grassland with very few trees. And grassland was cultivated for groundnuts, pepper and limited rice farming. But it was a home to rodents which multiplied and provided a good market for those who were skillful enough to catch them. People came to Fitia to buy dried or fresh meat and there was always an abundant supply of it. Kola nut was not a popular commodity although the earliest settlers planted some kola trees. They are the ones who had kola nuts and sold some quantities to outsiders making sure that some quantities were secured for the town's demand. The residents of the town operated on a principle of town mates first and others last in trade. This principle ensured that when they bought anything from another town it was not in their town and it worked.

Benakie came to Fitia more often to carry out his assignment rather than to buy kola nuts. He knew quite well that previous purchases of kola nuts were not worth the time spent going there.

He spent some time going up and down the streets shouting kola, kola but actually looking for attractive young girls in the houses along the streets.

He arrived at a house where he was shown some kola nuts to buy with two young girls playing at the side of the house. He bought the kola nuts and sat down on a long bench in the verandah. He called upon the taller of the two girls. She came to him in a hurry and stood by his side.

"Please give me some water to drink", he said smiling. The girl ran into the house and brought a cup of water. He received it and drank every bit of it.

"Do you want more?" asked the girl politely.

"No, thanks", he said, observing her closely.

He felt she could be a good candidate. She was beautiful and if her breasts were anything to go by, she was matured but timid to stare directly at him. She took the cup inside the house and came out looking on the side of the verandah to avoid his gaze. She ran briskly across the gutter to join her friend on the side of the house.

He waited until her father came back from his bedroom where he had kept some of the kola nuts that were not good enough.

The two men sat together and discussed a range of issues of common interest.

"Is it true that there are people in Duma who find it difficult to have a single meal a day?" asked the man rather baffled.

"Yes", he said.

"There are a lot of them in Duma sleeping in the market places, abandoned buildings, under the bridges, etc.", he continued.

"Why can't they come and work on the land? They will not be rich but they will have enough to eat and sleep in decent houses", the man said, with certainty.

"They are looking for office jobs and some have spent years waiting for those jobs yet they have not come. There are others who walk up and down the streets with less than a handful of rings, rat traps, one or two necklaces, a few watches, as a full preoccupation", he explained.

"Why can't the authorities of Duma encourage them to come to our region and engage the land?" said the man.

"The authorities are overwhelmed by their sheer number and don't know where to start", he continued.

"I will rather stay here on my plantations than to be in the city doing odd jobs and receiving paltry income.

Besides, if a healthy man cannot properly lodge himself what will be the future for his siblings?" asked the man.

He agreed with the man that if a healthy man decided to choose a market place for his house then his future was bleak.

"Do you have relatives in the police force or in other institutions in Duma?" he asked further.

"I don't have anybody in the police force but I do have a cousin working in the bank", said the man boastfully and smiling.

"When he takes his annual leave he writes a letter to me indicating the period he intends to stay with me", continued the man.

Benakie became cold from within on hearing what the man had to say. His chances were dashed and he felt he had wasted a lot of his time. His main condition for selection was not fulfilled. He felt he must leave immediately. He got up and bid them farewell and departed with his sack of kola nuts on one shoulder.

It was a bright sunny morning in Kambaya. The harmattan winds blew across the town carrying with it an irresistible cold that forced many to sit around burning fires at various locations in the town.

But as the intensity of the sun light increased, the fire spots were abandoned leaving the fire to burn the wood away until the next morning when additional wood was added.

Kaimoto and his wife sat around their own fire in front of their house.

"Don't ever tell anybody that I hunt chimpanzees? It is now a crime to hunt chimpanzees", Kaimoto said, with seriousness.

"Think properly. It is you who hunt them and distribute the meat to neighbours and if you don't hunt them the meat will not be available to me and to our neighbours as well. It is you who must stop hunting them, especially now that it is a crime", said Tenja with fear in her voice.

"You are right, but Sanagu is paying a lot of money for chimpanzee hands, feet and private parts to carry out his work. You will recall that one day I brought a lot of money and gifts to you after a chimpanzee parts' transaction in Seneun", he explained

"Yes, the chimpanzee that caused a stir and occupied the mango tree. Indeed you brought a lot of money", confirmed Tenja.

"Tell me, to what use are the chimpanzee parts to Sanagu?" asked Tenja.

"Sanagu is a fortune teller and diviner and those parts help him to make concoctions for his clients to help them acquire wealth or to get political power" he told her.

"Please stay away from chimpanzees. You have said that it is now a crime", warned Tenja.

"Look Tenja, we don't have money. Let me strike two more times and then I will stop", he concluded with desperation in his voice.

"But please make sure you do everything in the bush and don't bring any meat to town", she warned again.

On that note he got up and went to his bedroom. He came out well prepared for a hunting trip. He knew the time the chimpanzees came out of their hideouts to warm in the sunlight. He went through the back door into the garden and then disappeared into the bush.

He stayed there for quite some time and came back home very late at night and knocked door a few times and waited.

She opened the door without waiting to see who was there. She knew quite well that it was her husband but was not happy that he came very late. She went back into the room and sprang on the bed and turned her face to the wall.

He came into the room and greeted and she managed to reply in words that again showed her disapproval of his lateness.

"Tenja, learn to appreciate my efforts. All that I am doing is to ensure that you are comfortable at all times", he said annoyed with her behaviour.

She got up and brought the table closer to him and then raised the thick blanket that covered the food on another table. Within seconds she got the food ready on the table.

He smiled and commenced his dinner. He enjoyed the food because it was hot as if it was just from the fire.

"Tenja, you are a good wife despite your lack of trust in me", he said smiling.

"I trust you, but when you are late in the bush you keep me under unnecessary pressure", she told him frankly.

"It's OK; I will not be late again. But let me inform you that I was late because when I went into the bush and succeeded I decided to go straight to see Sanagu instead of coming back home. You know it is a long distance", he said as he drank a cup of water to end his dinner.

He then opened his bag and brought out the sum of two hundred and fifty thousand Leones and displayed them on the table. "This is what I got out of the journey", he said, pushing the money towards her. She received the money, thanked him and handed it back to him for safe keeping.

Kpaku's second meeting with Abu and Senga was under a coconut tree, a short distance away from the town. He looked forward for that meeting and when he received a message from Abu relating to the meeting, he received it with great joy indeed. He wished the meeting was for the same day. He believed that his status was going to improve once he became the campaign manager. His mind was fully occupied with the thought of his elevation throughout the day. He slept very little that night and got up early the next day to be in the meeting on time.

Kpaku sat opposite Abu and Senga and he was very anxious to hear something positive, something that would bring him fame and money.

Senga stood up and broke the silence by clearing his throat in an unusual way.

"We are here to make a significant appointment for the post of campaign manager. This appointment is based on proven record of hard work and commitment to duty in the community. We had on our list many individuals for the post but only one person was considered. And that person is no other than Kpaku", he announced and then shook his right hand vigorously while Abu clung unto his left hand.

"From today you are my campaign manager for Malenka. You will have a vehicle to yourself to reach out to all the youths in the region. And with you, I am confident that I am the next Member of Parliament for Malenka North", he said and waited for Abu's comments.

But since he was pensive and did not make any comments immediately, Senga spent some time praising his father for saving Malenka at a crucial moment. He emphasized the point that since he was a replica of his father both in appearance and character his appointment as campaign manager was not a mistake. It was based on how he carried himself in the community.

Kpaku was full of anxiety. He stood up and thanked him repeatedly again and sat down. He could not find the words to express himself. He looked completely lost in his thoughts as he analyzed the challenges ahead of him. He felt his chances of success were very good because of the cordiality that existed between him and the youths in the entire region. He did not entertain any doubts in his mind about the obstacles ahead of him but he was confident to overcome them. He considered the appointment as a stepping stone to success and would not allow himself to falter at any stage in the implementation process. His chain of thought was broken when Senga stood up again and cleared his throat to make another pronouncement.

"I have been assured that I am the next Member of

Parliament for Malenka North. There is no doubt about that. But a certain condition must be fulfilled, and that condition is that I must offer a superior sacrifice which I am prepared to do at all cost. I am working on it right now and your participation is highly required. I know the kind of man you are and I have no doubt that we can achieve this goal together", he concluded, looking straight at him.

"Superior sacrifice?" he asked hesitating.

"Yes, a superior sacrifice, a sacrifice that is not a goat, a sheep or a cow. Yes, a superior sacrifice," he said, putting emphasis on the word superior.

He understood the superior in his statement to mean a human being and that made him sick internally.

He felt heaviness in his legs and his stomach boiled over. He tried to brave it by keeping his face straight and without showing any signs of fear, but he could not control his feet, hands and stomach. All of these moved randomly and his stomach continued to boil over. Within a few seconds sweat dampened his shirt both on his chest and back. From his head, sweat descended unto his face as if water was poured on his head. He kept his hands busy wiping his face each time the downpour was heavy. He looked up and found that the two men were waiting on him for his comments. He tried to make a speech but his mouth refused him the words. He opened his mouth but the words could not come out.

Then he realized he was showing weakness even on the first day as a campaign manager, and so he searched the words quickly and stammered "I..., I am fully with you as far as your political ambition is concerned. I support, support you" he stammered and hung up.

Senga saw the fear in him but ignored his observations altogether because he was quite sure he would adjust to the news with time.

On his way to his house Kpaku continued to feel weakness in his legs as his mind was still on the sacrifice. He could not concentrate on anything other than the spillage of human blood which happened to be part of his new assignment. Why would he kill another human being for any reason other than at war? When he was young his father told him on many occasions how he over powered rebels and killed them, but the region was at war at that time and his father was justified. He analyzed the issue persistently in his mind but he could not find enough reasons to walk out of the deal as he had already accepted some money from Senga.

Besides, he feared for his life. If he leaked the secret or failed to go along with them he knew something terrible may happen to him.

Baudu was equidistant between Kambaya and Madina. It was a fairly big town with a growing population of youths and young adults. It was a farming town surrounded by forests which tended to cover the entire township. The youths in their cleaning up exercise cut down the giant trees that were prominent in the forests and exposed the town to more light. The town itself was dominated by the Essequi family with a unique tradition which had its headquarters in a northern town of Tako. The soul and spirit of that region was in Tako and the people looked forward to it for their prosperity in farming and in other endeavors.

When a senior member of the society was seriously ill he was taken to Tako for some sort of psychological treatment but news about the patients remained "critically ill" even after many years.

At the end of every six years the new and old members converged on Tako for a celebration that rocked the region. It was during that celebration that the Queen of the society, Kumba, the beautiful one and the King would come out and dance to the joy of members and guests.

The new members in their hundreds with their heads clean shaven and barefooted would then be allowed to walk through the region, speaking to no one but to themselves and feeding on anything they laid their hands on. Tradition afforded them that right and both members and non-members bore the consequences of their actions until their graduation which normally took place at the end of three months from the date of intiation. Previously, it used to be six years.

Baudu was an important town for Tesseh fishing. It was a unique type of fishing where a sloppy point along River Sumunji was chosen as the fishing site. Then, heavy logs were placed on both sides of the river to concentrate the flow of water in the middle. Slightly below the logs, a fortified bank was made across the river with a few outlets. Across each outlet, strong fishing nets were placed to catch any object passing through. Through these outlets, all kinds of fish, crocodiles or pythons were caught whenever they swam to the sloppy edge where the high water current forced them down the traps. The catch was always good and that was what made Baudu economically viable.

The concept of Tesseh was still in Baudu but the individuals who worked hard on them were either no more or were very old and weak. Therefore, the Tesseh was relegated to history and that made fish a scarce commodity in the entire region.

Benakie slept in Baudu. He had been there many times on his kola mission. After walking through some streets, he normally took a position in a house where he received kola merchants, and bought the quantity that he thought was good enough for his trade.

"Don't mind the dark sports on my kola. The spots can be cleaned off with proper washing in water", said a merchant whose sack of kola nuts was rejected.

"You could have washed them properly before coming out here", he said, determined not to accept any kola nut that was not properly processed.

By mid-day he was quite satisfied that he had bought enough kola nuts. Truly, his mind was not so much on the kola nuts but on his assignment. From Fitia to Kambaya he had not made any progress. In Kambaya he had found beautiful girls but their parents had relatives working in Duma. If that condition had not been there he would have got somebody already. But he recalled quite clearly that Senga emphasized the point that the parents of the girl must not have relatives working in the police force or working in big establishments in Duma. That was indeed a difficult condition. He found out that no matter how small a village was there was a relative somewhere in some big towns or in Duma. Some people told him that they had relatives in Duma but they could not say whether they were working or not and that made is assignment much more difficult. He felt that Senga would ask him to refund the money because it appeared he was not going to succeed.

In Baudu he was hopeful because he had already seen a lot of young girls in very poor homes. His assumption was that if those people had relatives working in big establishments they would have helped to improve their living conditions out there.

He tied his sacks and kept them in the verandah and walked around for a brief moment. He came back to the same point where he kept his sacks and found a young girl taking instructions from her parents as they left for their farm. The girl was asked to stay in town and cook for the workers who had already gone to brush their cocoa farm.

She took an empty bucket and ran to the river to fetch water.

Benakie waited patiently to engage her on her return. He felt he had got an opportunity as she was alone in the house. He took his chair close to the kitchen and waited. She came back, set the fire and commenced cooking.

She was tall and good looking. That was all he saw of her because she was busy moving in and out of the house, bringing out items relating to the cooking.

"What is your name please"? He asked, smiling.

"My name is Sundu," said the girl moving the mortar from the house to a spot close to the kitchen.

"Have you been to Malenka before?" he enquired.

"No, I have never been there. I hear quite a lot about it and it is my desire to go there and see the crowd, the market and the different types of dresses," said Sundu frankly.

"Most of your colleagues have been there. Why is it taking you too long to achieve that?" he asked.

"I am waiting for my own time and when it comes nothing is going to stop me", Sundu said.

"Would you mind if I create an opportunity for you to go to Malenka?" he requested.

"I don't mind at all but it will depend on how you are going to arrange it," said Sundu

"Well, it is simple. To go to Malenka you need some money to buy a few items that will appeal to you. I am ready to provide the money at any time you are ready to make the trip, obviously on a market day," he said again.

"Thank you very much for the offer but you have not said everything about the arrangement," remarked Sundu.

"I think it is a simple arrangement. Your friends have been to Malenka and you too would like to see Malenka. Anybody can understand that easily and permit you to go", he continued.

"You are a stranger, aren't you? If I have to take money from you for my trip, don't you think my parents should know?" asked Sundu, busy pounding some cassava leaves in the mortar.

He searched his mind for words in his defense but he could not find the appropriate words to defeat her argument because she was logical and reasonable.

"Well, leave the rest to me. I will find a way out as I make future trips out here. Anyway, do your parents have relatives working in Duma? He asked with interest.

"Yes, my uncle is a serving police man in Duma", said Sundu.

The sound of a policeman sent another set of shock waves that symbolized failure. Was he ever going to find somebody without relatives in Duma? Could one succeed with a nebulous and extended family structures? These questions occupied his mind constantly and he felt that the condition that no relatives should be working in the police force or any big establishment in Duma was unrealistic. He wondered why he did not question that condition and request its removal right at the beginning.

Discouraged, he brought out his two sacks of kola nuts from the verandah and got somebody to help him with the extra sack to Madina

'Once upon a time, said Panga, sitting close to Mina.

"No Panga, allow the children to settle down properly and make sure you raised the wick of the lamp to give more light to the group," Said Mina.

The children came into Mina's room and sat down, anxious to learn a new story.

"Once upon a time," said Panga again.

"The pig discovered a very small but hard nut which was hard to crack. It was brownish in color with two holes on the side for germination. The sample was taken to the king and all the animals were assembled the next day to discuss what they thought was an important discovery. None of them could say precisely what it was and where it came from.

The monkey came and observed it carefully but he could not say where it came from or what its use was. All the animals, from the elephant to the mouse came but failed to provide any information that could be used to identify it correctly.

Then, hare came and examined it. He knew something about it but feared that he may be punished for speaking the truth. He moved some reasonable distance away from the crowd and said, "My friends this nut is "Tau". It will germinate and grow into a tall tree and produce thorny branches with beautiful long leaves. It will produce oily fruits especially for those who are able to climb it. But its leaves will also produce fine threads which can be made into small ropes which will be used in traps to catch animals," Hare said confidently.

Elephant was angered for such pronouncements which were baseless and without any proofs and shouted, "Bring me the biggest and strongest rope from anywhere in the forest", said Elephant, rather furiously.

The pig just turned around and saw a "Fonomoeh" rope and cut it with his strong teeth, drank some water that dripped from it and brought it forward. Elephant held it and tore it to pieces. "If the strongest rope has a fate like this", pointing to the pieces, "then Hare's rope has no place in our kingdom. The fact of the matter is that Hare talks too much. Please bring him forward so that he can tell us more about it", requested Elephant.

But hare had made good his escape.

"You want me to continue?" asked Panga "Yes", said the children.

"The animals then banned Hare from all subsequent gatherings. And the word "Tau" was considered satanic and banned from use. The sample was dumped in a nearby swamp and all the animals were asked to disperse," continued Panga.

But hare was in a hideout close by and heard everything they said. When they had all gone he came out of hiding and identified the spot where the 'Tau' was dumped.

He visited the spot very often when it was safe for him.

After a long time he went to the spot and found that the 'Tau' had germinated and grown tall with its thorny branches spreading around it. He could not speak to any animal about his findings as he himself was in hiding, but he was determined to be present somehow at the next meeting. He sat down and planned well what to do to attend the meeting and without wasting time went into action. He dug a tunnel right up to the meeting spot and placed in it connected tubes of the branches of a paw - paw tree which he would use to speak to them from his hideout. He opened up the tunnel to the meeting spot and placed leaves on it to conceal the exposed edge.

Meanwhile the leaves of the "Tau" tree had matured and a certain man had already used the thread-like substance to prepare traps which were positioned along the river banks and across the paths of some animals.

And within a week Pig found the young son of deer dead by the road side. He examined the deer and found that his feet were in ropes. He took the deer and all the items that were responsible for his death to the meeting spot. An alarm was made and all the animals assembled at a short notice.

Right in the center of the meeting laid the young deer with ropes around his feet and the trap sticks tied to the ropes. The young son of deer was stone dead.

"Cut the ropes around his feet and bring them forward", cried Elephant aloud.

The ropes were cut and passed from one animal to another for examination.

All of them knew exactly what had happened. It was the 'Tau' but it was a crime to pronounce the taboo word.

"What can we do about this?" asked Elephant.

The cow, goat and sheep came forward and suggested that animals needed peace with man, the trap setter. They suggested that a team should be appointed to meet him and find a way forward in the human and animal relationship.

"What?" said the leopard? "You want to take us into slavery? You want man to tie ropes around our necks and tether us on trees in his garden? No, no, we will be independent and we are not prepared to make peace with man," the leopard pointed out.

"What should happen to our friends who want peace with man?

"Chase them out," shouted the crowd.

The cow, goat and sheep were chased out to the towns where they have remained permanently.

When they re-assembled there was a high pitched voice like a loud speaker warning,

"Tau is death to the animal kingdom, it is everywhere, and the animal kingdom is doomed."

"Look around and arrest hare for breaking the law," said Elephant, furious over what he considered satanic pronouncements.

Suddenly, a trap went off and caught a bush cow at one end of the meeting. Another went off and caught a young Pig. Both animals fought desperately to free themselves from the grip of the traps but to no avail.

Every animal looked to Elephant to do something positive but instead he allowed the two animals to battle it out by themselves.

"Both pig and bush cow are good fighters. We want to test the strength of the ropes on their ability to fight back and free themselves", he told them.

The crowd watched the two animals until they lost the last modicum of energy and died shamefully in the full view of every animal.

"It is sad to see our strong men die this way. They were very obedient and hardworking gentlemen. In fact, they are heroes and we'll always remember them and keep this day as the day of the heroes. Their deaths tell us that the ropes are a danger to some animals and those animals must be careful which paths they use," Elephant said.

The monkey and chimpanzee were furious over what had happened and came out and spoke boldly.

"Let's call a spade a spade. The rope which came out of the 'Tau' is a danger to the entire animal kingdom", they said fearlessly.

"What must we do for our protection?" asked monkey and his uncle chimpanzee.

"You too have broken the law by pronouncing the satanic word tau. What must we do to our friends who have bought the concept of Hare?" asked Elephant.

"Chase them out", cried the crowd.

All the monkeys and chimpanzees were chased out. They ran with all their might and climbed the tall trees deep into the forest and made the tree tops their habitat for life.

While all these events enfolded at the meeting spot, hare had already brought big black ants. He put them on the tree where Elephant's tusk rested. The ants climbed the tree and moved from the leaves to the tusk and bit it at various points. Elephant cried in pain and moved about rubbing his tusk on the ground and against tree trunks. The more he did that, the more he took additional ants and the more the pain increased.

The crowd was amazed at what was driving Elephant mad. There were no ropes on his feet yet he was in great pain, knocking down trees that stood in his way. The pain became unbearable and the thought of a river came to his mind. He ran a few kilometers away looking for a river and screaming in pain.

When he left the meeting hare came out of the tunnel triumphantly and addressed the crowd. He told them that 'Tau' was real. He pointed his finger at the dead colleagues as a proof. For the survival of the animal kingdom, he asked them to follow his instructions. He ordered that all animals with strong teeth engage the nuts everywhere and crack them. All the rodents must engage the young plants and stop their growth by eating their branches and uprooting them. He warned that all animals must learn to fly over the protective fences made by man around their rice farms and animals with short legs must dig under those fences to avoid walking into the traps. The pigs took the challenge to crack the nuts while the rodents agreed to bite off and destroy the young plants.

Despite his size, hare was made king and oversaw the successful cracking and uprooting operations.

Elephant lost his kingship and became a lone man but agreed later that 'Tau' was real and that all animals must come together to fight it jointly. He also warned all elephants to keep their tusk in trees and away from black ants.

This is why pigs and the rodents are still cracking nuts and destroying the young plants," concluded Panga,

"Good," said the children as they dispersed to their various houses with a new story.

Mina walked side by side with Panga until they arrived at the point where they thought the distance was equally divided between their houses. They stood face to face with each other and said good night.

Chapter Four

The catch

Benakie slept in Brima's guest room. Before they went to bed the two men sat in the sitting room and had a lengthy discussion about people, life and places. Mattu listened to the discussion as she too was wide awake in the bedroom which was opposite the guest room.

Brima was impressed by Benakie's life. A life of a sojourner, pushed around by the forces of demand and supply for kola nuts. He wished he had a piece of work that took him to various towns like him. He did not know many places and had not met many people in his life. He had never been to Duma and was not familiar with the way people lived out there. His closest relative that lived and worked in Duma died before he was 15 years old, and so he could not go there for fear of getting lost in a very big town. Besides, he heard that life was difficult in Duma with healthy people begging on the streets. He abhorred that type of life and would not like to go out there and end up being a beggar even for a single day of his life. He preferred Madina to many towns that he knew because it had plenty of farm lands and a lot of other opportunities. He has stayed in Madina for all his life and was fully engaged in farming. It had not been very profitable but it had never failed him.

He was born in Madina but his parents came from the north and he made sure that once every two or three years he went home to see relatives. His parents never made it a point of duty for him to know his grandparents and when they died his father never took him along for both funerals, making him a complete stranger to his extended family out there.

When his father died some years later none of his relatives came for his funeral ceremony. Despite that, one day he went home to get his relatives to know him but the trip was not fruitful because many people didn't even know his father, not to talk about him. He tried to create a link but it remained a very loose link which broke eventually because nobody made a return visit to him.

He met his wife mattu in Madina who also hailed from the north.

Unlike Brima, Mattu returned to her parents at the end of every harvest season. And each time she went, she took either Panga along or one of the two younger children.

The next morning, Benakie sorted out his kola nuts after breakfast. He packed the good ones untouched by weevils into one sack and the rest into a smaller sack. The partially damaged ones he gave away to Brima and his neighbours.

Then he requested that Panga should help him with the smaller sack to Malenka.

The request was not unusual. Boys and girls shuttled between the two towns often without any incidence and the to and fro journey lasted only a few hours if they did not take more time playing on the way.

Brima and his wife endorsed the request and asked Panga to return home immediately after depositing the sack in Malenka.

Benakie and Panga began the journey early to ensure

that she returned home in the day time.

He was satisfied that he had got his friend's daughter to be Senga's second wife. The marriage would strengthen his friendship with Brima and the entire family. He was quite convinced that she would be much more comfortable with a middle income husband in Malenka.

As they walked to Malenka he turned once or twice to assess her maturity and he was quite satisfied that she would be a wonderful wife because he felt that she had all the qualities of a good woman.

During the journey Panga realized that she had not informed Mina about the trip. Anyway, she felt she would give her a big surprise in the evening when she returned home. She was going to watch out for new things or ideas from Malenka for discussions with her. She loved Mina so much because she was kind to other children and knew many stories. She wished Mina would stay in Madina on a permanent basis. But Mina had told her she was in Madina only for the initiation ceremony which normally took place at the end of the harvest season. And most farms had been harvested in Madina implying that the initiation time was nearer. She wished both of them would be in the same camp so that she would learn more from her before she returned to school.

They arrived in Malenka in good time. They did not rest anywhere during the journey to ensure that her return journey would be quick and safe in the day time.

On arrival in Malenka, Benakie bought her some food and while she was busy eating, he went to Senga's house and briefed him and he returned in haste to keep her company. The two of them discussed frankly the new things that she found of interest in Malenka.

While they were busy talking, there was a knock on the door and a man entered and greeted them. The man happened to be Senga, who came to see her and to decide whether she was suitable for a second wife, in accordance with his agreement with Benakie. After exchanging greetings, he sat close to her and asked for her name.

"Panga is my name," she replied without much interest.

"You are indeed a beautiful lady. I am looking for a wife and you are just the type I am looking for. Do you mind being my wife?" Senga asked smiling.

"I am not looking for a husband but if you think you really want a wife, my parents are in Madina. You have to go there and discuss with them," she advised, trying to eat up her food quickly to begin her return trip.

"I am OK with all of that, but please accept this from me for now", he took fifty thousand Leones ($10) from his pocket and and pointed it at her.

"No thank you, I don't accept money from a stranger", she said and gulped a cup of water.

"Panga, accept the money. He is my friend, I know him very well," Said Benakie.

She then cautiously accepted the money but did not show any enthusiasm for it.

Senga tried to ignite a discussion but she spoke very little on any subject that he brought forward. Then, he bid them farewell when he realized that she was not happy talking to him but promised to see her in Madina.

Meanwhile Senga had positioned Abu and Kpaku close to Benakie's house to identify her before she left for

Madina. They took a position where Benakie would not see them but they could see clearly anybody who came out of his house.

So, when she came out of the house and stood in the verandah, they saw her from their hideout and ran quickly ahead of her on the road to Madina.

Benakie gave her some money and some items for the younger children. He escorted her across the town, passing through the market which was virtually empty. He wanted to ensure that she had a reasonable view of some streets of Malenka.

They went across the town and came to the road to Madina.

Benakie patiently explained to her the different sections of the town, the main routes to it, and the different sections of the market.

The journey to Malenka was not strange to her. She had been on that road before with her friends but that was a long time ago when she was much younger .She was shocked to see how Malenka had grown over the years and she was quite satisfied that she had got enough information to share with Mina in the evening.

He escorted her over a long distance and felt she could do the remaining distance safely without him. He then stopped and bid her farewell and sent greetings for her parents.

She thanked him for coming that far and assured him that she was comfortable with the remaining distance.

When he left, her mind went straight to the man who met her in his house. She felt Benakie was looking for a wife for him because when he came into the house he spoke directly on marriage and it was after Benakie had left her alone for some time. It was likely that he went to inform him about her.

She was shocked when he asked her to accept money from a stranger. She did not like the man because he was tall and lacked formality in his approach. She felt marriage must start with parents and relatives and then lastly with the one who was directly concerned. She wished she would not see him again.

She looked at the waning sun and felt she had enough time before nightfall. She increased her pace and she noticed sweat on her arms but the cool wind that blew in the opposite direction kept her comfortable and refreshed.

As she looked ahead of her she saw two men coming from the opposite direction but she did not know them. As they came closer she confirmed that they were not people from Madina.

Finally, they met and exchanged greetings.

"Are you the daughter of Brima and Mattu of Madina? Asked one of the men.

"Yes", she said cautiously.

"We have a message for you. Your mother had asked us to tell you that she is bringing items to Malenka tomorrow and she wants you to stay with Benakie until she comes," said the man.

"But my mother told me to return immediately after depositing Benakie's load and this is exactly what I am doing," she said.

"Look here," said the man, "We delayed our journey to my farm just to give you this message because we had assured your parents that we will make sure we see you and pass on the message", said the man.

"Well, I have heard the message but I am now very close to Madina and I am determined to complete the journey," she said with desperation in her voice. But the two men continued to engage her and would not allow her to proceed. They stood there and argued for a long time without any breakthrough and it was getting late. She did not believe their story but wondered how they got the parents' names right and even spoke about Mattu's planned visit to Malenka to sell some items which she was quite aware of.

How did they get the pieces of information if her parents did not speak to them? She pondered. She realized it was late and the two men had put fear in her. She could no longer walk to Madina alone because the men had put fear in her. She realized she was in big trouble and she wished some familiar faces would come along and free her from the desperate men.

But it was almost too late. One could no longer see the hair on the skin. Her heartbeat increased as they began the return journey to Malenka. They walked along the main road for some time and then branched off on a path which was supposed to pass through a farm belonging to one of the men. The path was also supposed to be a shortcut to Malenka according to the men.

Mattu hit her left foot against a stump and fell flat on the ground, returning to Madina from her farm. She did not pay much attention to the incident but she knew quite well that hitting her left foot was a bad omen. She tried to justify it by assuming that the foot paths were bushy after harvest because nobody considered it worthwhile to clean a path that would be abandoned shortly after a new site was selected for a new farm. She dismissed any suggestions that had to do with a mishap or some hardship.

She arrived home and found her two younger children playing in the verandah. They informed her that Panga had not returned home. The news pricked her like a sharp object in her flesh. She stood still for a moment reflecting on what might have happened to delay her return. So many possibilities ran through her mind but she was still hopeful that she would return as the sunlight had not completely disappeared. She sat down in the verandah with all her attention focused on the road from Malenka. She was there until nightfall but she did not return. She waited outside in the darkness until Brima returned and got the shocking news.

Brima and Mattu lay on their bed but without sleep. They expected a knock on their door and the voice of Panga but that did not happen throughout the night. They decided that Mattu should go to Malenka early the next morning to see Benakie whilst he would keep a close watch for her in Madina and its environs.

Panga and the two men arrived at an old farm house that was still intact but without any rice in it. On arrival, she spotted the tall man that met her in Benakie's house.

"So you are the one who sent these men to bring me over here. You are a wicked man. I have told you what to do if you want me for a wife", she said furiously

"Just cooperate with me and everything will be OK with you," he said, touching her on the shoulders.

"I will be OK when I see my parents. Please send me back to my parents, I beg you", she burst into tears and wept bitterly.

He went and sat close to her and wiped her tears away with his handkerchief.

Meanwhile Abu and Kpaku disappeared from the scene and engaged in some work a distance away under the cover of night. The sound of digging or pounding came from them but she was too confused to know what they were doing. Then, Senga held her hands and tried to bring her down on the floor mat and when she realized he was trying to abuse her, she put up a fierce resistance. They wrestled on the mat for a long time but he was unable to overpower her. She was strong and was determined not to give up. They continued wrestling and when he realized he could not handle her alone, then he shouted the names of Abu and Kpaku and immediately they showed up. They knew exactly what was going on and within a few minutes both men were on the scene helping him to achieve his goal. Without wasting time, they dropped her on the mat and held her hands and feet firmly.

Senga went into action and abused Panga for as long as he wanted. She screamed until she lost consciousness.

Abu and Kpaku left the scene to continue the work they were doing by the stream with the help of a bright searchlight.

She bled and lay motionless on the mat. She was exhausted and in extreme pain. Once in a while, she made unclear statements in her throat. But as she continued to bleed, she closed her eyes and her face went completely blank, but she was still breathing.

By mid-night the three men came back to the farm house and took her away and put her on a hastily made bed of sticks with four forked sticks at the four corners. Her feet and hands were tied to the bed and the sticks that made up the floor of the bed. Her resistance was not noticeable until her mouth was tightly covered. She kicked and struggled but under the grip of the three strong men, she could not do anything significant. Then, Abu opened his handbag quickly and took out a sharp shining knife. He held her throat firmly and with all his might pressed the sharp edge against it. Immediately, blood gushed out and landed into the basin placed directly under her neck. She shook and trembled and died quietly under the grip of three men.

Early the next morning, Mattu was already in Malenka. She located Benakie's house quickly and tapped on his door with vigor.

Benakie opened the door and to his surprise found Mattu in a confused state.

"Where is Panga?" She asked.

"She returned yesterday and I made sure I went with her a long distance away," he replied.

"You must produce her, you must produce her. She did not return to us yesterday, she is with you", said Mattu, shouting and crying.

A large crowd gathered in front of Benakie's house as Mattu dropped on the ground unconscious. Some elderly women came and took her away and gave her water to drink and poured some on her head.

Brima could not wait in Madina. He followed his wife and arrived in Malenka and found the crowd at Benakie's house. He looked around for his wife but she was not there. Then he spotted Benakie and went straight to him.

"Where is Panga? Tell me where she is or else I will kill you right now," he said. He held onto his shirt firmly and when he said that she returned to Madina the other day, Brima drew a knife from his pocket and raised his hand to stab him but many other hands held his hand in the air and removed the knife from him after quite a struggle.

Mattu then learnt about her husband and forced her way through the crowd and found him sobbing on the ground. She fell on him and the two wept bitterly.

They got up and moved swiftly to Mano to report the matter to the Mano police station, which was a substation to the Headquarters in Malenka. They made statements and were later detained for allowing their daughter to accompany a stranger.

By mid-day Benakie, his wife and some relatives that stayed with him were arrested and brought to Mano under police escort and were kept away from each other and from the public.

Before day light, Senga and the two men worked hard to ensure that the stream flowed back normally. They had derailed the stream initially while digging Panga's grave on the sandy river bed, to ensure that it remained a secret forever. After burying her, they opened the bank which they had created and the stream flowed over the grave normally and carried away the dirt that was created in the digging process.

They came out of the river and set a fire and burnt every item that had blood stains, including the bed of sticks. And in the farm house they removed every blood stain and burnt everything that could serve as evidence.

Finally, they burnt all the clothes they wore, including their foot wears.

They dressed in new clothes and each one of them took a different path to Malenka.

Within a day the police were in Madina where search teams were appointed and dispatched into the bush around Madina, Fitia, Baudu and Kambaya.

Also in Malenka search teams were already moving along the rivers and the forests. It was a comprehensive search and every town or village provided strong men to be in the teams. The search teams were advised to watch out for her in the forests, the farms and along the rivers. Each team had a gunman in case a leopard did the havoc and was prepared to carry out more attacks.

In Madina the voices of children playing in the neighbourhood could no longer be heard. The watchful eyes of their parents were constantly over them. They were monitored and strictly warned to stay indoors until the Panga saga was resolved.

Mina could neither eat nor sleep. She lost weight and her parents decided she must go back to school to get over the shock. Before she left Madina, she saw Panga in a dream, sitting in a beautiful hammock of gold. It dangled between two unique trees.

"Panga, where were you all these days? I have been crying for you day and night thinking that something serious might have happened to you," she had said joyfully.

"Stop crying Mina. I am now with my maker and I am OK. I have come to say farewell because you are going back to school soon," she said, smiling.

As Mina attempted to get close to her she disappeared and Mina woke up shouting Panga, Panga where are you? Her parents rushed into her room and enquired what happened. She narrated the dream exactly as it happened. The parents encouraged her that she was alive somewhere and she would be found one day. She was allowed to stay at home for most of the time under the watchful eyes of her parents, to ensure that whenever she thought of her friend there was somebody to encourage her by saying that she was safe and sound somewhere, although they were not quite sure where in particular.

The next day she got all her belongings ready and left Madina with an escort back to school. During the journey she wept each time she thought of Panga and the good time they had together.

Senga came back to Malenka and rested for the whole day. The next day he joined many others in the discussions relating to the missing child. His take on the issue was that a wild animal may have caused the havoc, citing the case of the leopard which struggled in a trap for many days and eventually freed itself and laid in an ambush for the hunter. And when the latter went to look at his trap a few days later, the leopard attacked and killed him. Many people knew about the story of the killer leopard already and were convinced that Panga's case was different.

In the evening he went to see Sanagu in Seneum to hand over the parts and a bottle containing the blood as required by him. He further gave him the equivalent sum of money for two cows in accordance with the agreement.

Sanagu assured him that he would be the next Member of Parliament for Malenka north and asked him to come back in a week's time to collect the magic belt and other items that will do the job for him.

He returned to Malenka to face additional challenges: The nomination was close at hand but the vehicle for the campaign had not arrived even though the arrangements were completed with his political mentors in Duma. Also, the number of contestants for the post had increased and the youths were still not properly canvassed. It looked as if he was still not in control and needed to do something quickly to put himself in control.

But key among his concerns was Benakie's statement at the police station. He needed to go there to know what he told the police. If he mentioned his name by linking him up with Panga for any reason, the police would definitely invite him and that would be a disaster for the project ahead of him. He felt that he must do everything positive to ensure that Benakie did not link him up with the issue.

The next day he sped off to Mano on his Motorbike. He arrived there in good time to do some enquiries. He went in and out of the police station many times and managed to get an idea about Benakie's initial statements.

According to his findings he was not implicated but the police made him a key witness, which meant that he was going to be interviewed more than once.

Senga was indeed a worried man. What could he do to stop Benakie from telling the police that he had asked him to look for a second wife and that Panga was the girl he brought to Malenka for the purpose? Moreover, if he told the police that he came to his house and that he gave her some money, he would be undoubtedly considered a suspect. To avert such a disaster, he made an attempt to see him once and for all but the police did not allow him. He realized the police were taking stock of his several attempts to see him and so he decided to leave the station and went in search of additional fuel for his Motorbike. He bought enough fuel for a return trip to Taya, a town to the north east of Tako.

Taya was situated by a big river called river Taya. Initially, it was a small fishing village but grew over the years into a big commercial town.

It was well known for crocodiles. In the dry season when the rivers dried up, crocodiles were spotted on the rocks that were exposed and strangers were not normally allowed to swim in the river because of the high incidence of crocodile attacks. But despite the attacks, the people of Taya were very skillful in catching them with nets and traps. That was why crocodile meat was available mostly in the dry season and most people came to Taya mainly for that purpose.

Senga arrived in Taya very late and asked a group of people to direct him to any successful crocodile hunter in the town. He was told that anyone who had a boat and went out fishing qualified as a crocodile hunter. It was based on his request that he was then taken to a young fisherman who had just arrived from the river.

"Good evening to you. My name is Senga from Malenka town," he introduced himself in a calm voice.

"I am Sosa, a fisherman and born of Taya," said the young man.

"I have come to buy some crocodile meat and some other parts," he said.

"Which part do you refer to as some other parts? You have to be precise, because I am tired and need some rest", said the young man.

"Please let us go to your house," he begged.

The two men walked a short distance and arrived in Sosa's house and sat down in his bedroom. "Honestly, I need some crocodile bile. You know quite well that it is medicinal and I need it for that purpose only," he said.

"It is against the law to sell crocodile bile. In fact, when a crocodile is caught the town chief must be in the know and the bile must be disposed of in his presence. As you may be quite aware crocodile bile is also a deadly poison and anyone found with it must pay a huge fine and that is capable of putting one's trade at a risk ", said Sosa.

But after so many appeals, Sosa sold a small quantity which he had kept in a small bottle in his ceiling. He sold it under oath that he must not use it to harm anybody and that nobody should know that he has it and that he got it from him.

After the transaction he rode back to Mano that night and arrived in the early hours of the morning.

Abu and Kpaku were already in Mano looking out for him. They brought good news that the long awaited vehicle for the campaign had arrived in Malenka.

They found him lying on the bed apparently very weak and somehow dehydrated. The news about the arrival of the vehicle did not move him as much as it did his friends. His mind was on Benakie's statement which could cause trouble for him but his friends seemed not to be aware of the relative importance of his statements to their project. He noticed that Kpaku's whole attention was on the vehicle and the campaign. He was already in the mood to address the youths and to be seen moving about from town to town. He seemed quite prepared for the campaign and to ensure that victory was theirs.

After much discussion, Senga sent him back to Malenka to receive the vehicle on his behalf and to recruit a driver with immediate effect. That was what he waited for, a decision that would touch on the vehicle and its use. He received some money for the operations cost and bade them farewell.

As Kpaku left, Senga closed the door on the two of them. He instructed Abu to pay somebody to prepare some food for Benakie and his family. He explained to him that there was a need to eliminate Benakie to prevent him from explaining what actually happened between the three of them.

Abu went out immediately in search of somebody that would do the cooking for a pay. He got a lady who was in great sympathy with the whole episode of the missing girl and the arrests and detentions of so many people who had nothing to do with the issue.

She received some money from Abu, got herself ready and departed to the market to get the cooking items required.

Meanwhile Abu went to the police station to ask for permission from the policeman in charge of the lockup that he was a friend of Benakie and that he was prepared to provide lunch for him and his family.

The policeman told him the time to see them and encouraged him to be on time; otherwise he would have to wait for the next day. There was not much time left, so he ran back to the lady to say that she must engage two pots and two fire spots. He gave her additional money and then left.

He returned to Senga and informed him about the developments. Senga did not make any mistakes about choosing Abu. He knew that he was active and effective and never said no to any assignment. He liked him and intended to make him the town chief of Malenka.

Later in the day, Abu went back to the lady and found the two basins of food ready. He put the basins into a basket and carried them to Senga's bedroom. And when they were quite sure that only the two of them were present, Senga produced the bile and put some quantities in one dish which was to be given to Benakie. "This is for Benakie. Don't make any mistakes about this. Make sure he eats the food in this basin and not that one," he indicated the difference between the two dishes clearly.

"There is a need to get rid of Benakie before he gives out information about my role in the whole affair", he informed Abu, making sure that he understood the instructions clearly before he left.

Abu quickly took the two basins to the police station and located the policeman in charge.

"I have brought some food for the detainees. The blue dish is for Benakie and the brown one is for his wife and others", he explained to the policeman who received each basin in turn, opened it and examined the surface keenly and put the lid on again.

He opened the prison door and called out the name Benakie twice, and immediately he came out and found him waiting.

"Do you know this man?" asked the policeman.

"Yes sir, he is a friend and a town's mate", he said.

"He has brought some food for you and your family," said the policeman.

"It is OK sir" he said to the policeman and thanked Abu for his efforts.

Benakie took his basin to an area of the station under the direction of the policeman.

The other basin was taken to where the wife and others were and both parties ate.

Abu waited for the dishes on a bench on the corridor of the police station. After some time the policeman brought the dishes back to him and he placed them into the basket again and took them to the lady after which he went to see Senga at his lodge.

The search for Panga was on-going in all the towns and villages surrounding Madina. The police officers charged with the responsibility of locating her pressed the teams to go further than where they had stopped preciously. All work on the farms had ceased as nobody was allowed to work until the girl was found. The forest, the swamps and the rivers were searched but she was nowhere to be seen. Nevertheless, the officers insisted on going further into the forests despite the fact that the teams were exhausted and fed up with the endless search.

The police officers interviewed so many other people in connection with Panga's disappearance but their main suspect was Benakie. They knew quite well if pressed further in future interviews he would disclose what he knew about her. They were confident that he was the key suspect and the officers were quite comfortable so far. They tried as much as possible to have more suspects and to push the search teams to do more to find her alive or dead.

The next day Benakie suddenly fell ill and lost his appetite. He coughed, complained of stomach pains and from time to time vomited. He ate very little and drank a lot of water. His condition was pretty serious and required medical attention. He was eventually removed from detention and allowed to see a doctor with a police escort. He was treated but his condition did not improve. He was referred to a more equipped medical centre but by the time the ambulance arrived there, it was too late. He had asked for some water and a cup full was brought to him. He drank some of it, after which he vomited, cried for help and then gave up the ghost.

The police officers had a closed door meeting with some of the suspects who were found to be innocent. They were allowed self bail on the condition that they reported weekly until the investigations were complete.

Then, the police spokesman addressed the waiting crowd, including people from Madina. The crowd came to confirm whether Benakie was dead because they knew that he was the key witness but his sudden demise would mean that the matter may be lost for lack of evidence.

The spokesman saw the tension and tried as much as possible to show that they were on top of the situation.

He informed them that Benakie was in good shape when he was arrested and continued to be active in detention. He ate well and never complained of any illness. He was never tortured at any one time by any policeman. He was scheduled for the next interview yesterday but it was cancelled due to his illness. His death was a shock to everybody including the police, he said to his audience.

He told them further that the cause of death was not known but the relatives were at liberty to request an autopsy. Shortly afterwards, the relatives came and asked for the body for burial. They argued that the suggestion by the police to carry out an autopsy would not prove anything and they were prepared to bury him and depend on the Almighty God to be their judge.

The request was granted and the corpse was taken to Malenka the next day for burial.

Most people remembered Benakie as the Kola nut man. His burial was well attended and some people came from the towns and villages where he did his trade. He was considered a kind and honest man. Nobody ever thought of linking him with the missing child and many people felt that his demise was caused by the shock of his arrest and detention.

Abu, Kpaku and Senga were at Benakie's funeral comforting the wife and children. They transported mourners to the grave site in the pickup van and back to Benakie's house after the burial ceremony. They played a very active role in the funeral ceremony and many people appreciated their kindness and love to the bereaved family.

Kpaku had recruited a driver known only as D-Man. He did not know his real name and did not do any background checks but accepted the name as it was. He explained to Senga that D- meant driver and so his name was Driver Man.

D-man drove them around and was very smart on the wheel and generally very active.

Kpaku was in control of the van as the campaign manager for Malenka North. He had met the youths and got their support for Senga. He was quite convinced that victory was theirs despite the fact that there was a keen competition for the political position. Nomination day was just a few days away and that kept him busy meeting youth leaders within and without Malenka. His desire to succeed as a good campaign manager kept him restless. He ate very little and hardly slept. He was always on the road with D-Man.

Brima and Mattu returned to Madina after their detention. Their house was full of sympathizers. Each time Mattu saw Panga's friends she could not contain herself but would sob and tears would run down her cheeks. Some elderly women sat around her and encouraged her not to lose faith in the search teams.

Her relatives from her home town had also come to sympathize and to take away the two younger children to their town which was far away and outside the zone of Panga's saga.

After many days, Mattu started speaking about her experience prior to Panga's disappearance.

"I knew something was wrong;" she told the crowd that came to sympathize.

"One day as I was returning home from my farm, my left foot collided with a stump and I fell flat on the ground", she told them.

"That was the sign," said one woman.

"Yes, an entanglement with the left foot and falling down flat implied bad luck," confirmed another woman.

As time went on, the sympathizers left for their various houses leaving behind only Brima and Mattu. She had the urge to go with her parents but she could not because they had to report to the police every week.

Chapter Five

The Consequences

Senga was ready to be nominated for Malenka North. He met the youths often and gave them enough money for food and drinks to keep them happy at the rallies.

A day to the nomination, he fueled his Motorbike and left for Seneun. He arrived at night as usual and found Sanagu in his bedroom, still busy doing some work for a client. He waited outside until he concluded what he was doing. When Indy announced to him that someone was there to see him, he opened the door immediately and Senga entered and sat down in one of the two chairs by the door.

"Welcome. I am sorry for the delay as I was working on a chieftaincy matter. A man came to see me yesterday because he wants to be a paramount chief", he explained.

"Is he from a ruling House?" Senga asked.

"No, but he will be crowned", he assured him confidently. At the end of their discussion Senga received a bottle from him containing some concoctions which he must rub on his face wherever he addressed voters and a long piece of cloth which was folded and sewn at one edge, which he must tie around his waist during the campaigns.

After receiving the objects he left immediately to catch up with Abu and Kpaku for the nomination.

He was quite happy that he overcame all the challenges that were a threat against his ambition to become the Member of Parliament for Malenka North. He was thankful to God for his choice of Abu and Kpaku and his political mentors in Duma who provided the pickup van in time. He was convinced that he was very close to power and more money, which would be good for his wife and children's education and welfare. He would acquire a piece of land in Duma and have a house built on it within a short time and increase the number of taxis to support his family in Duma.

He recalled that Sanagu had told him that a certain man would become a paramount chief even though he had no right to the chieftaincy. With his support, he would make Abu the town chief of Malenka the moment he became the Member of Parliament for Malenka North.

He rode back to Malenka with confidence and sped because he was quite familiar with the road network. Besides, he was under pressure to be present in Malenka hours before the nomination to hold meetings with the youths. He was close to Senke River and he ignored the step-gallop just at the foot of the bridge. He rode into the gallop and the Motorbike was lifted high-up in the air and went down on the rocks in the river. He landed with his head, with the Motorbike directly on his back. He cried for help because of the multiple injuries but there was nobody around to help him. The exhaust pipe of the bike burnt across his back. It was the dry season and the river was not that full to drown him. Part of his body was in the river and his upper body was on a flat rock.

Giant crabs came out of the river and made deep cuts on his body as he was unconscious. He remained in that position until the next day.

The time for nomination was a few hours away but Senga was not around. The election officers had arrived and the other candidates were already in the common room from where they were interviewed.

The youths for Malenka North were disappointed because Senga had not shown up. Abu and Kpaku rushed to Seneun where they expected him to be that morning. But unfortunately he was not there.

The nomination had started and it was at an advanced stage but unfortunately without him.

The youths then moved their support to another candidate who was initially thought to be an underdog. While the search for him was on-going, the nominations closed and by mid-day the unpopular candidate won the party symbol to contest the elections.

It was a young lad returning from his garden that saw a Motorbike in the river and reported the matter to his mother. She then contacted the youths who went directly to the bridge.

Senga was still in the same position with the bike on his back. The polythene bag that Sanagu gave him also had a bunch of keys and a laminated photograph of him. The bag got detached and floated downstream.

The youths arrived on the scene of the accident and found him in a terrible state. He was unconscious with wounds on his hands and feet and worst of all; he had some serious problems with his neck. He was rushed to the hospital where he was admitted.

The doctor in charge saw him almost immediately and carried out all the tests for which he had the facilities. Later in the day he called his relatives and informed them that he had multiple fractures on both hands and legs which did not pose so much threat to his life. He explained that he landed on his head and his spinal cord had suffered a serious damage. That was why he could not talk and that was serious indeed.

His hands and legs were put in P.O.P and he was made to sleep most of the time. His wife and children had arrived from Duma and sat in the corridor of the hospital. Each time the nurses passed by they would ask about his state and to keep them hopeful, the nurses told them that he was improving. He was in hospital for months without any reasonable improvement, especially with respect to his speech. He said things that did not relate to what he was asked and his response took a long time.

With their hopes dashed, Abu and Kpaku engaged the pickup van as a commercial transport. They chose strategic routes where the vehicle would be occupied throughout the day. At the end of each day, they shared good sums of money. Kpaku always maintained a higher share and for months the ratio remained the same way much to the disappointment of Abu who felt he was much closer to Senga and carried out crucial assignments than Kpaku.

He gave him some time to amend his ways but he remained inflexible, feeling that he was personally put in charge of the vehicle and any monies derived from it must be under his control and should determine who gets what.

Abu felt humiliated and decided initially on a physical fight with him the next time he gave him a lesser sum but he was not sure that by fighting and defeating him he would come to his senses and do the right thing. So, he decided to think of an alternative strategy that would eliminate him. Suddenly, his mind went straight to the remaining concoction that was used on Benakie's food. He recalled clearly where he had kept it and felt he had got the right solution to eliminate him.

He was aggrieved that Kpaku being the last recruit could treat him anyhow. He was next to Senga in rank and he should be in charge of the entire operation in the absence of him. He made up his mind that he would not accept Kpaku to act as a boss to him. As a matter of fact, he nominated him to be the campaign manager and indeed Senga listened to him.

In the meantime he decided to accept whatever Kpaku gave him while he worked on the use of the concoction to get rid of him once and for all. They worked together for a fortnight but the situation remained the same. Kpaku was inflexible to any changes and felt that he was the campaign manager and senior to Abu.

One day Abu wrapped the bottle containing the concoction and kept it in his hand bag as they set out on their trips. He could not use it throughout that day because the opportunity to use it did not arise. He brought it again the next day but could not use it because they always ate in a restaurant with so many people around them.

But one day they came too early and they were the only customers in the restaurant .When the food was served, Kpaku was busy doing some work on the vehicle outside the restaurant. Abu received the two dishes and by the time he came in, the deed was done.

Senga remained hospitalized with no improvements, but the doctors told his relatives a different story. But it was not difficult to know the truth when it was time for relatives to see patients.

His visitors were told either that he was asleep or a doctor was seeing him. Very little time was allowed to any selected members of the family to see him. One member of the family was fortunate to see him one afternoon. He wept when he saw him and gave him up. He told other members later that he did not recognize him neither was he able to speak to him coherently.

He told them that his case was a matter of time.

The doctors were not happy with him and made sure whenever he came to see him, he was told that Senga was asleep.

One day Senga did something which left every one baffled. He made signs with his hands and pointed in the direction of his accident. Nobody understood what he meant by doing that repeatedly whenever he had some consciousness.

He referred to the polythene bag which contained the bottle and the piece of cloth that were to give him political power and wealth. The bag floated down stream and got entangled at one point and stayed there for some days. But the dry season rains which were to cleanse the bush before the commencement of farming activities brought a lot of water into the river. The force of the water then dislodged the bag which continued its downward zigzag journey between the leaves and shrubs in the river. It went far down stream until it came to a point where the river divided into two small rivers. Then, the force which brought it down pushed it towards the river on the right hand side. It continued its downward movement on that river with the same difficulty it hard previously but it did not stop.

Kpaku asked D-Man to stop the vehicle half way through the journey to Tako. He came down the vehicle and tried to vomit but noting came out. A passenger advised him to drink some alcohol believing that it would help his stomach ache. One or two business people on board had cartons of hard liquor for sale. He bought a bottle and sipped it through the remaining journey to Tako.

Despite the use of the alcoholic drink, he did not get better. The pain in his abdomen continued to discomfort him to a point that he could no longer uphold himself.

Abu and D-man decided to rush him back to the Malenka hospital. On the way he became restless and D-man sped to arrive in the hospital before anything serious happened. He arrived in Malenka with his emergency lights on and broke the normal traffic rules by using shortcuts to reach the hospital in good time.

When the nurses saw the vehicle, they rushed towards it and brought Kpaku to the observation room. A doctor came over to the room to examine him immediately.

He shivered and sweat covered his body.

Within a few minutes he died quietly. The pungent smell of alcohol was all over his body.

The doctor initially concluded that the main cause of his death may be excess alcohol that may have caused a whole lot of problems in his major organs. He invited a senior member of his family into the observation room and he too was convinced that he drank too heavily as the smell of liquor was still over his body. The senior family member then organized a meeting with the rest of the family members where he told them that he and the doctor saw the corpse together and they found out that

Kpaku had taken excess liquor which may have caused his death.

The family members then unanimously agreed to bury the body and concentrate on the funeral rites than to engage in any investigations that may not lead to any useful findings.

The youths heard the news about his demise and learnt about the doctor's report which was discussed and accepted as fair, based on the circumstances of his death. They took a leading position in the funeral arrangements and worked closely with his family members who were in for an immediate burial. Once there was agreement on his burial the youths took charge of his body. They bought a coffin and worked with the family members to prepare his body for burial.

Before he was taken to the graveyard the youths put the coffin in the pickup van and made a tour of Malenka town followed by a large crowd of sympathizers. At the end of the tour the body was taken to the graveyard and buried amidst weeping and wailing.

After his burial, Abu and D-Man agreed to rest for three days to mourn the death of their friend. The next day they bought five twenty liter jerry cans of petrol in readiness for their future operations and stored them in Abu's house.

On the third day, Abu woke up but could not find D-Man and the vehicle. He believed that he took the vehicle to the riverside for cleaning. He waited for quite some time but he did not show up. Then he started to show some concern. He went around the town asking the youths whether they saw him with the vehicle but hardly anybody saw him that morning. He went everywhere in the entire town but did not find him and the vehicle. Could he have got instructions from Senga or his relatives to carry out some assignments? He doubted that very much because the relatives of Senga had kept secret every piece of information on him believing that somebody was bewitching him. In fact, they had already contacted a seer and he confirmed that a close relative was the main cause of the problems in his life.

Abu came to the obvious conclusion that D-man had escaped with the vehicle. He sat down to make up a plan to locate him. But nobody knew the driver's actual name and where he hailed from. He realized that he had lost everything. He was completely shattered by this discovery and he almost broke down in public. He reflected quickly how much would be lost if he did not show up. The loss was great and it would be a difficult matter to fight legally. He went to his house and wept bitterly under closed doors. He searched his pockets and brought out all the money that he had. It was not enough to sustain him for three days. Tears covered his eyes as he thought of the chances that he had with the pickup van. Would he ever see D-Man again? A question he asked himself often.

It was almost dark and so he went out and bought five bottles of hard liquor before the bar closed down business for the day. He also bought some cigarettes and a stick of candle. He felt he must drink enough hard liquor to stop tears running down his cheeks like a woman. He came back to his house and made sure he closed the doors and windows firmly. He believed that the wine would help him to forget what D-man had done to him and he did not want any neighbor to know that the pickup was no longer in Malenka.

He lit the candle and placed it in one corner of the parlor. He drank and smoked not just to stop his tears but to stop his mind going back to the incident. He drank until the five bottles were empty and smoke filled the entire house as if some cooking was going on inside. He leaned on the chair and fell asleep. The candle burnt and its liquid flowed until it reached the edge of the twenty liter jerry can in the corner of the house. When the candle finally burnt down to the ground level, the fire lit the liquid that flowed from it and the fire moved quickly to the jerry can full with petrol. Suddenly, there was an explosion as the can burst into flames and scattered everywhere in the house. Fire was on the floor, on the roof and in the rooms. The fire was thick and aggressive like the fire that burns rice farms in the dry season. By the time some people came out to help, the back of the building collapsed against the front, blocking the doors completely. The fire continued to burn the roof which caved in across the rooms.

The smoke was intense and Abu was in a drunken state and desperately trying to locate the doors or windows to escape the inferno. He cried for help but his voice was most often swallowed up in the burning flames. The fire burnt whatever was in the house. He tried to escape but he could not find the doors or any other opening that was big enough to allow his head to pass through. Then, there was another explosion, and yet another until all the cans caught fire and burnt down the entire house.

He could be heard screaming in the fire and the youths came with a ladder and leaned it against one corner of the wall which was smoky but without fire. They climbed it and sent down a rope through a hole which opened into the parlour from where they heard movements and cried to him,

"Tie the rope around you and we will pull you up," said the youths.

He held unto the rope firmly as the youths pulled him up. Then, half way through the distance the rope broke suddenly sending him back into the fire. His entire body was burnt and he was presumed to be lying on the floor of the house making some unclear noises

It was at that point of complete hopelessness that he gathered some strength and confessed aloud saying;

"Myself, Senga and Kpaku killed Panga for our political ambitions"

He repeated that statement to the hearing of most people that were present on the scene of the inferno. After sometime his voice could no longer be heard as the fire continued to burn until every item was totally consumed.

By the time a policeman arrived on the scene he was dead. He asked a lot of questions to confirm the rumors that he confessed that he and two others killed Panga. He could not get to the bottom of the matter because those who were present were afraid to speak up.

At the end of the day he invited two people who were the first to arrive on the scene.

The next morning, the policeman came back to the scene of the accident. He went into the burnt house and found Abu's burnt body. He also found broken bottles and elements of burnt pieces of jerry can and some candle wax on the floor. He noted everything that was of interest to him and then he went and discussed the issue with the community leaders after which the corpse was buried with a written permission from the police. But the pronouncements that he made before he died were considered serious. It was rumoured all around the town and the police wanted to get to the bottom of the matter but nobody wanted to be a witness. However, the deaths of the three friends, Benakie, Kpaku and Abu alarmed the entire town. Some felt that they were bewitched whilst others felt that they were being punished for some evil thing they may have done together.

The policeman had already invited two men who happened to be at the scene of the fire accident in which Abu was burnt alive. The two invitees were not happy because they were not ready to disclose that they heard him when he said that he, Kpaku and Senga killed Panga.

Nevertheless, they met to discuss what to say to the policeman whenever they were invited to the police station. After discussing the issue at length, they agreed between themselves that they should not speak the whole truth because if they did they would be considered key witnesses. Obviously, Senga's political mentors would hire lawyers to defend him and the lawyers would overwhelm any witness with a lot of questions. They would make him afraid, and cause him to make mistakes and appear to be a liar to the public.

"Look here my friend", said the first invitee, "If you are a key witness in such a matter you must be prepared to answer the following questions."

What is your name?

Do you know Abu?

Did you see him on the day of the accident? What were the colors of his clothes and the type of shoes he wore?

Did he make any statements whilst in the fire?

For how long did he make the statements?

In which area of the burning house was he standing when he made the statements?

If somebody hid behind the burning house and made those statements will you know the difference?

Did you recognize his voice?

What is the difference between his voice and mine?

In what language did he make the statements?

How well do you understand and speak that language? Did you learn the language or is it your mother tongue? What was your state of mind at the time of the accident?

Were you drunk or sober?

"And if one decides to object to some of these questions what will happen? Asked the second invitee

"The lawyers will shout saying, objections overruled. My lord, let him answer the questions?" explained the first invitee.

"And besides the avalanche of questions, the matter will stay in the court for years undecided. What is going to happen to your farm and to your family? Obviously, your family will starve because you will not do any effective work for all the years the matter will be in court" continued the first invitee.

The second invitee wholeheartedly agreed with the first that they should not speak the whole truth.

The next day the two men were in the police station and the interview started with the second invitee.

What is your name? asked the policeman.

Mbuine is my name, he said.

"What happened in your environment on the night of the last market day?" asked the policeman.

"I was woken up by somebody shouting fire, fire and when I came out Abu's house was on fire. I rushed there and joined the others to save him but we could not because the fire was too intense", he Said.

"Did he say anything while he was in the fire?" he asked.

"He cried for help to all around him", he Said.

Did he call particular names, he asked again?

"Yes he called the names of Kpaku, Senga and Panga", he said.

"Did he say the three of them, that is, Abu, Kpaku and Senga killed Panga?" continued the policeman.

"No, I did not hear that?" he said.

Why do you think he mentioned her name?" asked the policeman

"I don't know sir," He said.

No matter how he turned the questions around the answers remained the same for the two invitees. They had rehearsed their answers well to avoid serving as witnesses in court.

He then spent some time writing in his file what he made out of the statements made by the two men and they were later allowed to leave.

The next day, the policeman was at the hospital. The crowd was at the hospital too waiting to see a clear link established between the disappearance of Panga and the three friends, Senga, Abu and Kpaku. Every member of the crowd was eager and waited patiently until the policeman arrived.

He walked right across the crowd and went straight to the nurse where he requested to see Senga. The nurse in charge asked him to wait for a moment. A few minutes later, he was called upon and he followed her right across the main hall into a room where Senga sat on a bed. He had been on that bed since he had the accident and the nurses paid much attention to him because of the seriousness of his case. The nurses allowed the policeman to talk to him just for a brief moment.

While the policeman waited to get his attention he made the usual signs with his hands and pointed at a particular direction which proved to be the direction of his accident. He was still thinking about the polythene bag that was floating in the river. It floated a long distance downstream and finally got entangled in a web of sticks and ropes. It sat between the sticks and the ropes and the storm forced it to spin around. It contained thebody parts, the bottle, the bunch of keys, and the laminated photograph of Senga. It floated directly over the grave of Panga.

When the got his attention, he displayed the photograph of Kpaku before him and that action forced him to concentrate. He stared at the photograph curiously and waited to see what he would do next.

The next photograph was that of Abu's, and finally Panga's.

He opened his eyes wide and started foaming at the corners of his mouth. He vomited and then collapsed backwards on the bed. His condition suddenly became critical.

Then, the nurses pulled down the curtains around his bed and asked all visitors out of the ward.

The policeman went out and stood in the verandah and wrote copiously in his file for quite some time. Then he went through the crowd without saying anything to anybody.

A certain man from the crowd ran after him and asked, "Is he guilty?"

He stopped, turned around and stared condescendingly at him and walked away.

Then a senior nurse came out of the hospital to address the large crowd that had gathered outside the hospital. It was a crowd made of men and women acting on a piece of information that the police had got a clue to Panga's disappearance and that Senga was a party to it. The crowd moved towards her, expecting her to say something about the meeting between the policeman and Senga. When she got closer to the expectant crowd, she stopped suddenly and announced to them that Senga was resting and responding to treatment and that nobody would be able to see him under those circumstances.

"I am in sympathy with him. However, Can we please know what the police man said to him and what his reply was?' asked a man from the crowd.

"I am a nurse and as such I take care of the sick. That is exactly what I and my colleagues are doing. We are attending to the sick. Please go and ask the police man what he said to Senga and what response he got from him", she said and moved back into the hospital to avoid further questions.

The crowd lingered around for some time and then dispersed without getting any idea about why the police man came to see him. Some members of the crowd had a strong feeling that Senga knew something about the disappearance of Panga, which was why they wanted to know his role in the whole affair. They feared for the lives of their own children, especially when Senga was not a stranger but a close door neighbor.

Inside the hospital the nurses battled with Senga's life to bring him back to consciousness. They administered drips and mopped his body with cold water to bring his temperature down. When the drip was sufficiently administered into his body, he moved his arms and feet under the watchful eyes of the nurses. Shortly afterwards, he woke up and asked for some water. The nurses waited for the tube containing the drip to be completely empty and then he was given some water to drink. He drank a mouthful and then sat on the bed with the help of the nurses. He looked around as if he was in a different world and asked repeatedly, "who brought me here?" The nurses ignored his questions and concentrated on checking his pressure which read normal. Then he stopped asking and went into a deep reflection which caused tears to run down his cheeks. He remained in that mood for quite some time and then he began to behave in a strange manner: "I did not intend to kill her; I just wanted to become a member of parliament. Panga, don't torment my spirit, don't come near me, stay away from me", he shouted at the top of his voice and the nurses brought down the curtain around his bed and calmed him down. They put him back on the bed and spoke to him in low tones until he fell asleep.

In the hospital, there were two male patients who knew Senga very well. They were admitted close to Senga's ward and they heard clearly what he said concerning Panga and they were quite disturbed. They discussed and decided to pass on the pieces of information to their relatives that came to visit them in the evening. The next day the news was everywhere in the town that Senga confessed openly in the presence of the nurses that he killed Panga.

The news moved individuals and groups to the hospital day and night to see him and to confirm from witnesses what he said concerning Panga. They hung around the corridors most often and tried to engage some porters or nurses but without success. They kept coming and leaving the hospital without any additional information to what they knew already. Some of them went back home and began their own investigations to ensure that the truth of the matter was revealed and the criminals identified to put a stop to ritual murder in the community. They knew quite well that a policeman was handling the matter and they were quite aware of the consequences of interfering directly with the investigations but they did so to send a strong a message to all potential murderers. However, they took their time to discuss the issue with people whom they trusted and did so where it was absolutely safe to avoid a collision with the police.

The wife and relatives of Senga came under immense pressure from the public. Their family was discussed and fingers were pointed at them everywhere they went within the town. As a result, they met as a family and agreed that Senga must be removed from the hospital within the shortest possible time to put an end to the speculation that Senga was directly involved in Panga's disappearance and to put a stop to the incessant provocations. A car was hired to take him to Kamati hospital in Kamadu and his wife decided to go ahead and make all necessary arrangements.

By midnight, the driver of the car and his friend undertook the venture. All Senga's relatives stayed out of the deal to ensure that nobody knew who removed him and his whereabouts. That move was to remove him from Malenka on the belief that once he was out of sight he would be out of the minds of the people. Meanwhile, his family had already discussed with the doctor in charge and secured his discharge on a particular date and at midnight.

He was never aware of the decision to discharge him and was least prepared to move to any other town or village to receive his medication. He was hopeful that one day he will receive his healing and be a normal person again. And so when the nurses woke him up and told him that he was due to be discharged, he could not believe it until the nurses packed his suitcase and other items which he had on the shelf. Although he was unhappy about the arrangements, yet he looked forward to seeing some relative to take him home. He was very much disturbed when two young men appeared before him on the steps leading to the car. He shook his head violently as a form of resistance and refused to cooperate with the nurses. He kicked at them and refused to walk and cried for help, doubting the identity of the men. But he was sick and weak to resist any attempts to take him out. The nurses moved faster and got him into the back of the car. He hadn't got enough energy to shout to the hearing of the other patients in the hospital, although some of them who were awake by midnight may have heard him screaming.

When both the back doors of the car were firmly closed, the driver moved the car speedily and jolted it long the highway towards a private hospital in Kamadu, a growing rural town with at most twelve hours of electricity each day in key institutions. The two young men kept looking back to see their lone passenger at the back seat who sat up and waved, indicating that the driver should stop the car. But the more he did that, the more the driver sped on the half graded and half tarmac road. Finally, when he realized that his instructions were not obeyed, he gave up and fell back on the seat and tried to cope with the light and heavy gallops, some of which almost threw him on the floor of the car. But he held tenaciously to the remaining piece of the non- functional seat belt, the edge of which rode on the seat as the car surged forward.

The journey was long but definitely not tedious for the driver and his friend. They enjoyed the speed and the rock and roll motion of the car through the gallops and short hills which suddenly appeared before them. As for Senga, the journey was all painful and completely out of his control. He did not even know where they were going and he deliberately avoided asking about their whereabouts for fear of receiving an answer that might shock him to death. He was not completely speechless but he preferred to listen to get a clue of where they were going. His silence paid off because he heard one of the young men talked about Kamadu and Kamati Hospital which were familiar places to him. From the pieces of information from them, he knew the young men were taking him to the Kamati Hospital but he wondered who authorized them.

The driver slowed down the car as he approached Kamadu. It was dawn and the town had just woken up. Some children could be seen carrying buckets of water on their heads to their various houses. The car sped across the town trying to locate Kamati hospital. Finally, it pulled up in front of a big compound which had the name Kamati Hospital in bold letters. Immediately, Senga's wife, Saley appeared in front of the vehicle with two strong men at her back. They opened the car and took hold of him and carried him into the hospital, where the nurses received him in the outpatient section of the hospital

Saley paid the driver and then joined the nurses and the two strong men who also received some money and left the hospital. She returned to the room where her husband underwent medical checks. There was horror in her eyes as she approached Senga on the bed. Her gaze slid down from his head to his toes which were pale and dusty. She spoke to him through a haze of tears which crowded her eyes and flowed down her cheeks. She doubted the rumors that her husband killed Panga and she had to send her children away to prevent them from getting a clue about the rumors in the town about him.

Back in the hospital in Malenka, the other patients woke up and found Senga's bed neatly dressed up with no evidence of him anywhere within the hospital. They looked at each other in doubt and concluded that something was wrong somewhere. One of the patients was so inquisitive that she went to a nurse and asked what happened to Senga. The nurse looked at him from head to toe, and her breath hissed out between her teeth unconsciously, and then she said "Discharged" without showing any interest in the issue. He went to his ward with the feeling that Senga may have died but could not understand why she was not speaking the truth. The other patients tried as well to enquire about his whereabouts and they too were told that he was discharged but they remained unconvinced. They wondered why he was not discharged in the morning or in the afternoon but when every patient in hospital was asleep and very late at night.

By the end of the day Senga's disappearance in the hospital was part of the news making the rounds in the town. And immediately there was a surge in the number of visitors to the hospital to confirm that indeed Senga was not in the hospital and to find out where he was.

The hospital's management team gave new instructions to the security men to refuse entry to anyone that came in respect of Senga. Suddenly, the main gate area of the hospital became crowded as the security men carried out their instructions without fear or favor. But the crowd melted away as soon as a police man in uniform appeared suddenly at the gate on nobody's invitation but to see another patient in the hospital. His presence was completely misunderstood by the agitating crowd. He calmed the crisis just by asking for order in the management of the gate much to the happiness of the hospital staff

After a month's stay at Kamati Hospital, Senga was much better; the bruises on his sides and legs healed up and the pain in his neck subsided significantly. He was allowed to walk around the hospital as a form of exercise to ease the stiffness in his legs. He did the exercise for a week and felt even much better.

But very early one morning he made a strange noise on his bed and the nurse in charge went to see what was happening and to her surprise she found him screaming and fighting off some unseen person:

"Panga, don't come near me .The fire around you is burning my skin. I did not kill you single handedly, please leave me alone", he cried out with his feet kicking and his hands in a boxing position.

The nurse was shocked and became completely speechless. She went quickly into the doctor's office to draw his attention to Senga. Within minutes the doctor and other nurses were around his bed listening to him.

'' Panga, forgive me. I wanted to be a member of parliament for my constituency and I was advised that I must kill a girl to succeed and the lot fell on you. Stop tormenting me. Go to Kpaku and Abu", he continued shouting and fighting off the unseen person.

Without wasting any time the doctor checked his pressure and temperature and found them normal. He carried out other checks and was fairly satisfied with the results. He then asked the nurse to invite whosoever brought him to the hospital.

She recalled quite clearly that a young lady brought his breakfast about 9 am every morning. She informed the other nurse who had just changed shift that anyone who brought food for Senga must see the doctor in charge.

Fortunately, it was Saley, who came with the breakfast that morning. As soon as she arrived in the ward, a nurse came and led her to the doctor in charge after a brief discussion.

As she walked closely behind the nurse she wondered what might have happened to cause the doctor to request her presence with immediate effect. She was quite aware of the progress Senga had made over the last few weeks. Could it be some additional medicine that he wanted for him? She wondered. Before she got into other thoughts they were already before the doctor.

"Please have a seat. Are you Senga's wife or a relative?" he asked and put away the diary in which he wrote.

"I am his wife", she said with worries on her face.

"Good to know you madam. I have called you in connection with your husband's illness which we have managed well to the best of the ability of the medical team. I wish to say that he has recovered in accordance with the tests carried out today. However, I witnessed a scene this morning that showed that he has developed some psychological problems and the solution for that cannot be found with us for now. I have asked you to come because I have decided to discharge him today", he said. While the doctor was busy talking to her, a nurse rushed in and whispered to him. Quickly he asked her to come along and led the way through the wards to Senga who was busy making other pronouncements.

"Please bring me the bottle that was found in the plastic bag that was found on the site of my accident. It contains Panga's blood and it is for my use to become a

Member of Parliament for my constituency", he made his confessional statement repeatedly in the presence of his wife and many patients and nurses.

"Madam, do you understand my position now?" the doctor asked her.

Emotion crowded her chest as she heard the confessions of her own husband in public. Her face went blank and she cried out aloud, sat down on the floor of the room and ran her hands through her hair unconsciously. She did not know what she was doing at that moment until the doctor stood before her and offered her a free transport to take her husband back home. Later, he was given some sedative to get him to sleep and to release the seeming psychological pressure on him. The sedative put him to sleep almost immediately and the journey back home commenced in earnest. It rained heavily for most of the time, slowing down the vehicle to an incredibly low speed. But as they approached Malenka, the rain slackened to an aggravating drizzle which forced the trees along the road to bow down to it. The ones that resisted it had their branches broken off and forcefully taken to other spots. That too slowed down the vehicle and made the rest of the journey boring.

When the vehicle arrived in Malenka the drizzle kept the neighbors at home and consequently nobody saw the vehicle or the passengers. Nature was so kind to Saley by making sure the neighbors did not know that her husband had arrived home. She was tired and completely frustrated by Senga's pronouncements. Could it be true what he said? She had never known him to be a liar and he always spoke the truth no matter the circumstances. So, when he said he and others killed Panga, there was every reason to believe him. If he took part in Panga's death could he be a trusted husband? These thoughts flashed through her mind as she and the driver took him into his bedroom.

Very early the next morning Senga woke up without showing any signs of weakness. His wife sat by his side and tried to restrict him to the room. That worked for the early part of the morning but when he requested to visit the rest room, he could not be refused. And when he went outside the house to the rest room which was at the back of the house, the neighbours saw him and wondered when he came back to the town.

Back in his bedroom, he recommenced his narrative on Panga, after his wife and close relatives failed to stop him. They closed the doors and windows but his voice was distinctive, clear and loud for anybody in the neighborhood to understand what he said. That brought all his neighbors to his house and everybody heard him say that he, Abu, and Kpaku killed Panga.

Two days later, two police vehicles sped across the town, their lights flashing and their horns blaring as if the policemen were chasing a criminal. Some people, out of curiosity followed the two vehicles to see what was going to happen and surprisingly they found them parked by

Senga's house, with some policemen both the back and front of his house. Senga was still inside his room and the policemen asked him to come out but instead he continued saying that he and two others killed Panga and that he organized it.

On hearing what he said, the police produced an arrest warrant and showed it to his wife and then moved swiftly into his bedroom and arrested him. The crowd wanted to hear more about how they killed her but the police whisked him away into the police van and moved away.

In the police station Senga's behaviour was not completely normal. However, he made a long statement about where they precisely killed Panga, the body parts they removed from her and where they buried her in a stream. He also gave the name Sanagu, the diviner who advised him to sacrifice a female, preferably a virgin to fulfill his ambition to be a Member of Parliament.

Two days later, the Local Unit Commander of Malenka Police Station, in conjunction with the pathologist, put a team together to test the validity of his statement about killing and burying Panga in a particular stream which he vividly described. The team composed of energetic young men with pickaxes, machetes and shovels on board one vehicle whilst the pathologist and some police officers were in the other vehicle. They drove slowly towards Madina as the road was narrow, rugged and bushy. After some time, the police officer in one of the vehicles asked the driver to stop where there was a footpath near the only cotton tree on the right hand side of the road. The driver watched for the cotton tree and stopped immediately when he saw it and asked the passengers to disembark. Then, he and the other driver parked the vehicles and followed them on the footpath to the old farm.

Already news about the search for the remains of Panga by the police had leaked to some the stakeholders in the region including Panga's parents who were advised by their relatives to deliberately stay away from the search.

The policeman who had complete information on the murder led the way to the farm and down to the stream where she was supposed to have been buried. The stream hadn't enough water because the dry season was just about to end. The officers came together and checked the details in the booklet and then instructed the young men to brush a particular area along the shallow stream.

The young men were many and physically fit, and within a short time there were no grasses or shrubs along that part of the stream. The policeman further instructed that a gutter deeper than the stream be dug by the side with the hope of emptying the stream into it. Some of the young men bragged that they had done illicit diamond mining in Kono District long ago and that the job was not a difficult one.

They began the job with tremendous zeal to demonstrate their skill and to see the remains of the little girl whose death had negatively affected everything they did in the entire region.

As the digging and shoveling continued, a crowd started to gather around the workers on both sides of the stream. The police officers were not happy about their presence but it was too late to ask them to go away. They allowed them to stay on the condition that they joined the work force in any capacity to make the job easier. And immediately the workforce doubled and water started trickling down into the gutter from the stream. As the work progressed the stream was forced to abandon its course and emptied itself into the gutter, exposing the river bed completely.

The LUC and his men went down on the sand left

behind by the water, did some measurements and asked the workforce to dig cautiously in accordance with the marks they made on the ground.

The workers divided themselves into two groups; one group digging from the north and the other from the south, with a distance of about twelve meters between them. They dug the entire width of the stream to ensure they did not miss anything substantial.

The crowd grew and the late arrivals happened to be mostly women who stood aside watching the process with keen interest and not to miss any step in the recovery process. So, they monitored the mud delivered by the shovels and when a pick axe was trapped between stones or ropes, they went to see what held it.

They continued like that until one of the young men announced that his shovel touched a strange object. Immediately, the crowd moved onto his side but the police officers prevented them from descending into the stream. The young man made the hole bigger until a long whitish substance showed up clearly. The pathologist went to the site with his hands in gloves and examined what came up. He completed his examination and walked up to the LUC and whispered to him that it was a human bone.

The women noticed the conspiracy and did not wait to be told that it was the remains of Panga. They wept bitterly and the noise went far and wide and attracted the attention of other passersby who also joined the team. The digging stopped temporarily to allow them to cry out their bitterness and hate against Senga. Some shouted "Senga is a devil that must not live" and the young men said boldly that if Senga was released from police custody for any reason they would deal with him severely in their own way.

The LUC then asked them to step aside and warned that nobody should jump to the conclusion that the bone found belonged to Panga until it was ascertained by the doctor. They stepped aside and the digging continued under the supervision of the pathologist. The remains were intact and recovered wholly. When it was finally removed and placed in a white piece of cloth, there was weeping and wailing.

The young men moved the corpse quickly into one of the vehicles and without wasting time the vehicles sped away one after the other leaving behind a lot of mourners.

The crowd eventually broke up and went away to their various towns and villages, spreading the news that Panga's remains were discovered where Senga killed her. The news made rounds quickly in the entire region.

Brima and his wife Mattu wept but not for too long because an elderly man came to them and said "You must stop crying because your God saw your tears and made the criminal to confess exactly what he and others did in secret and showed where they did it. It is only the spirit of God that can move criminals to confess their crimes openly. Be patient and continue to trust your God". From that moment, they sat in the veranda and received many people who came to sympathize with them.

Three police officers in plain clothes were already looking for Sanagu the diviner. He was supposed to be in Seneun but news of his involvement in the murder of Panga sent him running away to unknown destinations and the police were on his trail. He went to Fakia and told his friend out there that he was sick and came to see an herbalist. He spent the whole day indoors eating very little. But by the end of the second day the news was in Fakia as well that Senga and Abu killed Panga on his advice. From his bedroom he heard and saw some people discussing the issue and pointed fingers at the house where he lodged. He felt he was the subject matter of that discussion and decided he must move as quickly as possible but it was still day time and he did not want anybody to know the path that he would take.

So, he waited until it was fairly dark and then he sneaked out of the house from the back door and disappeared into thin air barely before the team of police officers arrived in Fakia and went straight to the house where he lodged on a tip off. But when they arrived there they were told that he was there in the afternoon but disappeared suddenly without saying anything to anybody.

Sanagu was on the run and he knew within himself that death hung over his head. The arrest and imprisonment of Senga and the manner in which the entire community reacted to his involvement in the murder meant that there was no hiding place for him. However, he felt he did not kill Panga but advised that Senga needed a sacrifice in order to become a Parliamentarian. If he went ahead and killed somebody what was his business in that? He felt if he could find a good lawyer he could be freed if he was ever going to be prosecuted. Indeed, the possibility existed that he could be freed, especially if he gave a lot of money to the lawyer. But would the community ever forgive him? He pondered.

These thoughts flashed through his mind as he walked to another village where he felt the news about the issue had not been heard. He walked a long distance and arrived at Katay River which was close to Kambaya. He undressed and took his bath and rested to enjoy the cool breeze that blew from the tall trees that formed a fence along the bank of the river.

He was terribly hungry as he walked up the small hill on the top of which Kambaya was built. Then, suddenly he heard the town crier and stopped instantly to understand the message that he was giving out.

"Men and women of Kambaya, this is an important piece of information for every household, so please pay attention. We all know the young girl Panga who disappeared from Madina some time ago. It has been found out that three people killed her; Senga, Kpaku and Abu, on the advice of Sanagu the diviner. Kpaku and Abu are dead and Senga who made the confession has been arrested and Sanagu is on the run. The police at Malenka who are handling the matter have instructed each and every one of us to arrest him and hand him over to any police station in the region. They have assured us that by law every one of us has a right to arrest a suspected criminal and hand him over to the Police. It is based on this instruction, every one of you is mandated to arrest him anywhere you come across him and hand him over to the chief as a temporary measure, after which he will be handed over to the Police. If anyone lodges him or fails to carry out this instruction, the matter will be between that person and the Police" the town crier said and moved to another section of the town.

Sanagu almost collapsed on hearing the measures taken to arrest him. He walked back in the direction from where he came and went into the forest to ensure that nobody saw him. He went deep into the forest and ended up in an old farm with a broken farm house where he made himself comfortable for the night. He felt he must go back home and hide in the thick forest round about his garden, from where he could harvest some cassava and bananas. But suddenly it occurred to him that even his wives and children had been authorized to arrest and hand him over to the Police or Chiefs. He concluded sadly that there was no longer any hiding place for him on earth. Tears ran down his cheeks as if a shower had been opened over his head. He got very little sleep because he had constant fear that he might be discovered by someone, and also due to the giant mosquitoes which harassed him throughout the night. He moved from the farm house before the first cock crew and followed a path that took him far away from the towns. He knew the area very well and he was confident that nobody would be out there that early.

He was dirty and rough but he had no time to look at himself. His mind was focused on how to avoid prosecution and death. He did not kill Panga directly but he knew within himself that he implied a human being when he told Senga that he needed a superior sacrifice and that was why he was on the run. He regretted having chosen a profession that put the lives of girls and women on death roll.

He fed on wild fruits in the day in his hideout and a human voice sent him running in the bush like any squirrel, and his body became adapted to thorns and bush blades. He was losing his humanity very fast but he had to live in the bush and he survived on fruits.

The Police combined Senga's confessions and the forensic test results and charged him for murder and transferred his matter to the High court in Duma. He appeared before the judge some days afterwards and not only pleaded guilty but explained in details how he raped her and killed her with the help of Kpaku and Abu. The Judge examined his behavior in court and realized that he was not normal and adjourned the matter to another date to give him enough time to be psychologically stable.

Meanwhile, the LUC invited the parents and the stakeholders of the community about Panga's funeral and explained to them that Senga had been charged for murder and the Police were tracing Sanagu. A date was agreed upon on which the body was to be released for burial at Madina. The police offered two vehicles to convey the body and mourners to Madina.

The stakeholders in the community went back home and after a lot of consultations they came out with a huge sum of money being contributions from individuals, towns and villages towards the funeral. Out of the funds a provision was made for a befitting coffin and other funeral related materials. The balance sum of money from the contributions was given to Brima and Mattu, the parents of Panga, a decision which was unanimously approved by the contributors. It was further agreed that men and women from all towns and villages round about Madina should come out in their numbers to bid Panga farewell and to show to her murderers that the community condemned their murderous act and will continue to resist them to ensure that their children were secured in the community.

Brima and Mattu could not believe their eyes when they received the huge sum of money. They thanked the community members for their concern and support and said that the new unity that the death of their daughter had brought should be sustained because they believed that if they had the kind of understanding and cooperation amongst them Panga would not have been easily trapped and killed.

The funeral arrangements went ahead with a regional force behind it. Food and lodge was arranged for people coming outside Madina and many youths volunteered to receive the body in Malenka and to accompany it back to Madina.

On the day of the funeral the youths left Madina so early that the first cock crow found them on the outskirts of Malenka. By the time the police team arrived at the hospital they were already there and ready to perform any duty. The representative of the community was called upon to receive the corpse, already in the coffin which was selected by their representatives.

The coffin was in the open police van with the youths guarding it whilst the other vehicle was reserved for the use of the elders of the community. Later, the vehicles took off and moved slowly along the rugged road to Madina with many mourners both at the back and sides of the vehicles singing farewell funeral songs.

Madina was full to capacity to the extent that there were not enough available seats in the houses to accommodate a large number of the youths who turned out for the occasion.

They gathered outside in small groups in various corners of the town and discussed the funeral in their own way whilst they anxiously looked forward to receiving the corpse from Maleka.

Suddenly and continuously, the horn of vehicles blared across the town, and the sound brought virtually everybody to the main road leading to Malenka. They were quite convinced that the corpse had arrived and they were quite correct. The two vehicles appeared far away in the midst of a countless number of people. The waiting crowd moved to receive them but two Police officers who led the way into the town made sure the highway was not blocked. The vehicles then moved slowly towards Brima and Mattu's house with the horn continuously blaring to signal the arrival of the corpse.

Mina had arrived and sat face to face with Mattu, consoling each other. When the vehicle carrying the corpse stopped, Mattu got up and walked towards it with her hands raised high above her head in sorrow.

"Welcome back home Panga. You left here alone but you have thousands of people escorting you home today. You left here unknown but today your name is everywhere around our community. You left here only with few friends but today you can boast of thousands. And today Mina, your best friend is here with you again to bid you farewell.

You were in hell under a stream but you have come home to rest at the back of your house.

Welcome, welcome my love and my darling", she stopped when Mina and Brima took her by her hand and led her away into the house.

Without wasting any time, the youths came forward and received the coffin and carried it gently to the grave site at the back of her house, where a huge crowd waited patiently to receive it. After prayers were offered, the body was lowered into the grave amidst singing and dancing to show that her death was a defeat for her murderers and their accomplices.

Food was served immediately after the burial and everybody ate to his or her satisfaction. While the service went on, a meeting for all was arranged in the open space in front of Brima's house. Chairs and tables from most houses were brought out and arranged in straight lines across the entire space to accommodate many people, especially the elders. The youths stood either at the back or on the sides and waited to see what the elders planned.

Suddenly, Brima stepped forward and two youths led him to the lone chair which was set aside from the others. He sat down in it for a moment until the noise died down. Then he got up and addressed the crowd.

"Brothers and sisters of Madina, mourners from other towns and villages, I thank you all for the love that you have shown to me and my family, to the town and to the deceased. I want to assure you that though I have lost Panga, the message that has been sent across the entire region is so strong that ritual murder will become a thing of the past because of the awareness, unity and cooperation that we have enjoyed together these few days. I am now going to be the keeper of my neighbour's children and all of us gathered here today must adopt the same principle to close the information gap between us. This will provide safety for our children.

I thank you once more, not forgetting the police whose crucial role we will always remember", he stopped and there was a thunderous applause followed by a familiar song which they sang together and danced to until night fall.

The search for Sanagu was ongoing but without any clues. Some farmers reported that they spotted a man running into the bush at a cross road. He looked very thin and rough and resembled him. The next day two police officers were dispatched to the area on Motorbikes. They crisscrossed the roads and some footpaths but they could not find him.

One day two youths rode a motor bike at top speed to Malenka from Fakia. They wanted to see no less a person than the LUC of Malenka police station. They arrived there and were taken into the waiting room. They were very uneasy and impatient. They walked around in the room expecting the LUC to appear before them without any delay. The LUC appeared later and invited them into his office where they informed him that they saw a man dangling on a tree in the forest a few kilometers away from their town. They emphasized that flies were all over him, implying that the body had decomposed.

The LUC and his men met under closed doors and at the end of the meeting a dispatch team of police officers was sent to the area including the two youths. The driver of the vehicle sped on the road to Fakia and arrived there in good time to walk to the site. The team was accompanied by the elders of Fakia to identify the corpse. They walked across rivers and streams and climbed a hill and then moved on a plain. At the far end of the plain was the tree on which hung the unidentified body.

They were greeted by foul smell when they approached the scene and were forced to cover their mouths and noses to avoid the offensive smell.

After close examination, the Police instructed two youths to bring the body down from the branch of the tree. The body dangled from a strong bush rope tied to the branch with a loop around his neck. The body was at an advance stage of decomposition. Two youths climbed the tree and cut the branch, causing the body to drop on the ground. Immediately, the youths identified the body as that of Sanagu and there was agreement from the rest of the team that knew him. But the body had decomposed to an extent that the police permitted his burial on the spot where his broken body laid. The youths ran to Fakia and brought the necessary tools for burial. The soil was soft and the digging was not very difficult. Within a short time, the grave was available. The broken body was dragged into the grave and it was neatly covered. Some land marks were placed around it for any future investigations.

The team of Police officers drove to his home town to break the news to his family but found the house completely empty. They were told that his wives and children left at the time when rumors became strong that he was an accomplice to Panga's murder. By the time the Police arrived back at Malenka, word had gone right across the community that he committed suicide to avoid arrest.

Senga's matter was the third on the list of cases to be heard at the first sitting of the High Court. His matter attracted so much public attention because of its unique nature that the accused pleaded guilty and provided adequate information that led to the recovery of the corpse which was buried under a flowing stream.

The court was full to capacity. There were representatives from Malenka, Madina, Fakia and other towns and villages from the region. The Police team from Malenka was there and sat on the side of the prosecution.

A large crowd gathered outside the court as there were not enough available seats in the court room. Everyone was there to set eyes on Senga and to hear from his own mouth how he raped and killed Panga. But what was amazing about the matter was that he had no sympathizers, not even his family members. His wife and relatives abandoned his house in Malenka the moment his confessions became public. He was alone in court and his defense lawyer cautioned him about his flippant statements but he admitted his guilt in such a bizarre manner that he angered everyone present in the courtroom.

His matter was called up and he was brought into the dock. He looked around the court room and then concentrated on the Judge before him. He wore the same shirt since his last appearance and he was rough and dirty.

The prosecutor got up and read out his crime and explained his confession and all that happened up to his detention. He informed the court that he used his confessional statements to identify the site of the crime and recovered the corpse from under a flowing stream.

There was murmuring both in and outside the courtroom when the public learnt that the corpse was recovered from under a flowing stream.

Senga interrupted the prosecutor and narrated exactly how he raped Panga and with the help of Abu and Kpaku, killed her, took some of her blood and removed some of her body parts.

There was weeping and wailing from the women when they heard the confession. The uproar caused some obstructions and delays to the court proceedings, but the judge had no control over the emotions of the crowd.

The jurors went into session and without much delay came out with a guilty verdict and a life sentence for him. Their decision was based on his confession and the adequate information which he provided to identify the site of the crime and the recovery of the corpse.

"Are you guilty or not?" asked the Judge, to see whether he was consistent in his confession.

"I am guilty", said Senga repeatedly.

The Judge informed the court that the incidence of ritual murder, especially that which concerned the girl child had become rampant and those behind it were usually people with political ambitions, in conjunction with some lazy and wicked people who referred to themselves as diviners. He said he agreed with the recommendation by the jurors to send him for life imprisonment, to send a strong message to all and sundry that human beings were created in the image of the Almighty and cannot be subject to any form of sacrifice, to the point of losing their lives.

Finally, he turned to Senga and pronounced a life sentence on him and asked for his reaction.

Senga looked around. His gaze went from one corner of the room to the other and fell on one woman he knew quite well.

"Tell my wife that what I have done I cannot undo; I killed Panga to be a parliamentarian", he shouted so that she could hear from the back of the courtroom. He behaved as if some hidden force was compelling him to speak up.

The Judge observed his behavior generally and wondered if he was not dealing with a mad man but there was no evidence of that in the file before him.

"Take him away", the Judge ordered, and he was removed from the dock to his cell.

"Court rise", announced a police officer, and then the judge went into his chambers and the crowd melted away from the court house in a happy mood because one murderer had been removed from their community.

Explanatory notes of exotic words used in the novel:

Banda (verb) - A Kono verb meaning to finish.
Fonomoeh (noun) - A Kono word for the biggest bush rope which is very useful to farmers for their construction work. It also contains a lot of water which some farmers consider pure for drinking.

LUC- Local Unit Commander of the Police Force
Mbuineh (noun) - A kono word for a rat with a long mouth (The carrier of Lassa fever)

.Nyanguma-   A Kono word for a cat.
Nyangumeh - A Koranko word for a cat.
San-nyo (verb) - A Koranko verb meaning to finish or to be absent.
Tau (noun) - A Kono word for a palm nut.

Tesseh (noun) - A Kono word for a unique fish trap which is set across the entire breath of a river.

Konos and Korankos are tribes of Sierra Leone and share a common border along the North- Eastern axis.
Twi- Twi- The sound made by rats

Kono District- One of the fourteen districts of Sierra Leone, famous for diamonds and Gold.